The Cowboy's Surprise Return

THE COWBOY'S SURPRISE RETURN

THE COWBOYS OF SWEETHEART CREEK, TEXAS BOOK 5

JEAN ORAM

The Cowboy's Surprise Return
The Cowboys of Sweetheart Creek, Texas Book 5

By Jean Oram

This is a work of fiction and all characters, organizations, places, events, and incidents appearing in this novel are products of the author's active imagination or are used in a fictitious manner unless otherwise stated. Any resemblance to actual people, alive or dead, as well as any resemblance to events or locales is coincidental and, truly, a little bit cool.

All characters and events appearing in this book are fictitious. Any resemblance to real people, alive or dead, as well as any resemblance to events is coincidental and, truly, a little bit cool. This includes the Sweetheart Creek mayor and his wife who are not based on anyone I know. Okay, I borrowed resemblances to their names in order to affectionately tease them a tiny bit. :)

Printed in the United States of America unless otherwise stated on the last page of this book. Published by Oram Productions Alberta, Canada.

COMPLETE LIBRARY OF CONGRESS CATALOGING-IN-PUBLICATION DATA AVAILABLE ONLINE

Oram, Jean.

The Cowboy's Surprise Return / Jean Oram.—1st. ed.

ISBN: 978-1-989359-42-6 / 978-1-989359-39-6

Ebook ISBN: 978-1-989359-40-2

First Oram Productions Edition: February 2021

Cover design by Jean Oram

A NOTE FROM THE AUTHOR

Cole appeared on the scene years ago in The Marriage Pledge. He kept popping up and I kept thinking his story was coming soon. Soon. Soon.

Several years and eight books later, here he is with his very own story! (His four brothers—and even his mother—really insisted their stories be told first.) I hope you have enjoyed the sneak peeks into his past through several of my other books, and that you "feel all the feels" as you read his long-awaited return home and happily ever after with one of my all-time favorite heroines.

With love,
Jean Oram
Alberta, Canada 2021

ACKNOWLEDGMENTS

Thank you Margaret Carney and Tessa Shapcott for your patience while I rearranged my schedule as I sent you numerous books over 2020. Thank you to my beta readers Margaret C., Donna W., Lucy J., Erika H., and Sharon S. for a reader's perspective on the long-awaited Cole's story. And to my error team—thank you once again for the polish!

To those who have been waiting for Cole's story since he first came on the scene in the small town of Blueberry Springs in the Veils and Vows series. Here's to Cole finding his happily ever after.

1

Yesterday

Cole Wylder leaned against a wood-paneled wall and took in his bustling welcome-back party. The Watering Hole saloon, a bar that smelled of beer and the great outdoors, was filling up as though he'd been missed in the five years he'd been away. Five years to look back on the mistakes he'd made in his hometown of Sweetheart Creek, Texas.

Namely, the ones with his ex-girlfriend April MacFarlane, who he'd danced with earlier without either of them committing murder.

He must be a changed man, after all.

However, despite rumors to the contrary, he hadn't come home to sweep her up in his arms, nor did he want her back. In fact, he had a strong suspicion she'd eloped with his younger brother Brant a month ago to thumb her nose at those rumors, as well as to prove she'd moved on.

And yet the gossip still floated through the air like mustard gas. Sometimes Cole felt he should pick up a fake girlfriend to help dispel those rumors, if not for his own sake, then for April and Brant's.

He hadn't known what to expect when he'd returned home, having such little contact over the years. If he was a betting man he'd have placed his chips on his father's continued cold shoulder, and April running him out of town. So far, only the former would have won him the jackpot.

He lifted his beer to his lips, the button-up shirt he'd found in his old bedroom closet pulling at his shoulders as if trying to hold him back. In his peripheral vision he caught a few people whispering about him, looking away when he met their gaze. Fresh starts weren't as easy as a person would think. He'd come home to mend fences, and turn away from the crazy things he used to say yes to.

No more putting the wild in Wylder.

Cole found himself glancing toward a table tucked at the front of the saloon where the long bar ended. Jackie Moorhouse was sitting alone, looking gorgeous in an off-the-shoulder top and smoky eye shadow that gave her a demure, mysterious vibe. He focused on the ceiling so she wouldn't catch him staring. What was it about Jackie that kept drawing him in? They'd spoken on New Year's Eve, as well as at his family's Christmas dinner, and it had been awkward and uncomfortable. She was a woman who brought sunshine and laughter wherever she went, yet he swore she had shadows, too.

Like him.

As his gaze found Jackie again, he reminded himself that he'd sworn off women until the summer. He needed to focus on his family and rebuilding bridges. That had been his plan in coming home, and seeing their reluctance to open their arms and fully welcome him had only reinforced it. He'd earned their reservation by leaving without a goodbye and then not staying in contact.

"Nice to have you back." Cole flinched when a slap on his shoulder left a stinging imprint. "Things were getting a little stale around here." Wade Ross weaved his way onto the dance floor, spun around again and stumbled against a table, spilling drinks.

"What happened to him?" Cole muttered to himself. The man used to be a pillar of the community, heir to a pretty swank family business and smart enough to tutor Myles, the second youngest Wylder. But Wade sure wasn't acting like a man who had it all.

"Did Wade say 'stale'?" his cousin Nick asked, coming to stand beside Cole as the latest song ended. He had a woman tucked close, the two of them out of breath from dancing. "Tell that to the sheriff."

"I'm sure he's enjoying some quiet," Cole said, thinking how far back he and Nick's troublemaking ways went.

"You remember Polly?" Nick asked, tightening his arm around his partner.

Cole guessed she was in her thirties, her posture hinting at a more refined life than her typical Texan cowgirl outfit suggested. Whatever her story, she seemed happy, and deeply in love. And it was obviously mutual. Cole's wild and crazy cousin, who'd vowed he would never settle down, looked as though he wanted to put a ring on Polly's finger.

How was it that everyone he knew had fallen in love—including all four of his brothers?

Had *everything* changed while he was away?

"Indigo Bay," Polly said mildly.

"Of course," Cole declared, as memories of summers away from the ranch flooded his mind. Nick and Polly had been inseparable as teens, while Cole had been chasing girls and sulking over missing a month of practicing rodeo back home. He'd received a few college scholarships but had never cashed them in, staying on the circuit and collecting belt buckles and trophies instead.

"How late does the party go tonight?" Nick asked.

Cole shrugged. He planned to leave long before closing time, and his old friend Trouble began sending out tempting invites.

"I don't want to babysit you in the drunk tank all night," Sheriff Conroy Johnson warned as he walked by, with several drinks clutched in his hands. "My granddaughter's birthday party's tomorrow, and I don't want to be a walking zombie and miss it all." He gave Cole and Nick a warning look.

"We'll be good," Cole promised.

The sheriff snorted and continued on.

"You two seem to have developed quite the reputation," Polly said, eyeing the sheriff as he doled out the drinks to a table of middle-aged folks sitting near the band.

"We did."

"But we're not like that anymore," Nick said quickly. Cole nodded in agreement. These days his Friday nights were usually spent home alone.

Cole found his attention drifting to Jackie Moorhouse again. The perky spitfire was still sitting by herself, looking uncharacteristically glum. April had suggested he go talk to her when they'd been dancing earlier. Possibly his curiosity had shown? Or maybe it was related to the numerous well-meaning people who had hinted rather blatantly that Jackie had a crush on him and had been waiting for him to return. If that was true, she should be in the CIA, because she was hiding her feelings very well.

"Hi, Cole," Daisy-Mae Ray said, fluttering her lashes as she joined their small circle.

"How are you still single, Miss Gorgeous USA?" he asked, turning on the charm.

She laughed. "You're still not interested?"

She'd been one of the first women to approach him when he'd come home, and therefore the first to be turned down. He gave her an apologetic smile and shook his head. "I've got to mend some fences before I can get serious about a woman."

"I wasn't suggesting anything serious," she said, stroking his shoulder, her subtle floral perfume drifting over him.

"Sorry, sweetheart."

"In other words, no women, because he's leaving soon." Nick gave him a glance to confirm, ever the wingman.

Cole shook his head. "I'm staying."

Daisy-Mae rolled her eyes. "Sure you are. Keep me in mind if you get lonely."

He touched the brim of his cowboy hat, his shirt pulling again in the process, as she turned to melt into the crowd. She was Myles's ex-girlfriend, and even if Brant didn't respect the bro-code regarding brothers and their exes, Cole did. Although Brant possibly got a pass on hooking up with April, seeing as he'd had a thing for her since they were preteens, and if Cole had been around he would have given them his blessing.

He swung his attention once more to the woman sitting in the shadows near the door. Why wasn't Jackie surrounded by her usual gaggle of giggling friends, or hanging out with April? Why was she sporting a serious frown that made her almost unrecognizable?

Where was her joy tonight?

Come to think of it, where was his own? This party was for him, after all. He turned his attention back to Nick, who was asking if his beer needed a refill. He shook his head with a thanks, trying to sort out where he fit into this town that never changed, but seemed to have done so in his absence.

It was time to rewrite his life, and for some weird reason, it felt as though Jackie held the key to how he was supposed to do that.

* * *

Jackie was done. She'd been sitting off to the side, pretending to have a good time, for almost two hours. Sure, she'd floated from table to table occasionally so people wouldn't think something was up, but she'd mostly stuck to herself, sorting through her moods. All she could think about was the fight she'd had with April on their walk over to The Watering Hole, and how her friend took love for granted.

April had called her a chicken for not throwing herself all over her long-time crush Cole Wylder as soon as he'd stepped foot in Sweetheart Creek again. But anyone could see that his years away had weighed on him, and that he wasn't the same man who'd left town. It was right there in the haunted glimmer in his eyes, available for all to see.

Jackie sighed and swirled the drink she'd been nursing all night. Like a fool, she'd continued to carry the burden of her childhood crush even when Cole had disappeared for five years. Now she wasn't sure the man she'd dreamed of for so long still existed.

To make matters worse, she realized that April had been right: milk did last longer than Jackie's boyfriends. She was just a flirt the local men didn't consider as marriage material. So what had she done? She'd pinned her hopes and dreams on a man who didn't do serious or long-term.

Hopeless.

No wonder April had been so cavalier about telling her to throw herself at Cole. And maybe the reason her words had struck so deep was that they'd hit upon some truths Jackie had been hiding from herself for too long.

She checked the clock on the wall, figuring she'd been at Cole's welcome-back party long enough that she could politely leave. After all, April and Brant had left an hour ago, their expressions dark. They were going to have a blowout fight, neither of them realizing just how good they had it. Stuck in their own drama, they couldn't see the relationship gold they were sitting on.

It seemed like every time Jackie turned around, her friend had effortlessly ensnared another man. But this time it was true love, and April taking it for granted made Jackie so frustrated she wanted to shake her. Whereas Jackie wasn't sure she'd ever truly been in love, despite her thirty-two years living in a town full of matchmakers—herself included.

Maybe it was envy?

The fight with April had at least reinforced what she already knew. If she was looking for love—which she was—that meant no more flings. They were nothing but diversions, something to hide behind so she didn't have to deal with the scary idea that true love might not be waiting out there for her.

Jackie downed the last of her drink, tracking Cole Wylder, the man of the hour, as she did so. He was still hot. Still had that fluid, confident way of moving that made her want to sigh in satisfaction every time she saw him.

She'd been chasing him for as long as she could remember. Him. Just him. Sure, she'd flirted with his brothers, but that had simply been to ensure she didn't freak Cole out with her steady, pinpointed interest.

She set her empty glass on the small table and stood.

It was time to bid that old crush farewell and move on.

Jackie collected her jacket from the back of her chair, then moved to the door, smiling and waving, putting on the Jackie Show as she went. She'd had to work at sitting alone tonight, giving herself space to cool down after the fight with April, as well as sort out her true feelings about Cole. Sometimes a gal just needed to sit and think. But if the town got to know that was the real Jackie, the quieter one who wasn't a trouble-free flirt, she wasn't sure where she'd fit in.

As she neared the exit she turned to take one last glance at Cole. He was shaking hands with someone she couldn't see through the crowd, that slightly haunted look flickering in his gaze. The man was still all brawn and devilish smile, coupled with that intensely quiet way of looking at a person, making her feel like a shaken bottle of soda that was ready to fizz over at any moment.

"Jackie!" called Karen Hartley, pulling Jackie's attention away from Cole. The local librarian was beaming, having just been ensconced in the arms of Myles, the second youngest of the five Wylder brothers.

"Your lipstick is smeared," Jackie informed her, wincing as she shifted from foot to foot. Her arches were protesting tonight's choice of footwear, a pair of high heels instead of her usual cowboy boots.

"Oh!" Karen quickly dabbed at her mouth, blushing and appearing happier than Jackie had ever seen her. Love looked good on her.

"Hey, are you free on the thirteenth and fourteenth?"

"Of February?"

Karen nodded.

Jackie shrugged, swallowing the lump of loneliness that had formed in her throat at the thought of Valentine's Day. She'd planned to spend it, a Saturday, at her father's nursing home. Even if he didn't always remember who she was, the cookies were good and the stories the other elders told tended to be entertaining, although a bit repetitive.

"I guess so. Why?"

"The library's thinking about holding a fundraising event."

"You need volunteers?" Jackie perked up. Helping out would be a great excuse to be busy if anyone asked if she had a date for the most romantic day of the year.

"No, we need fun people to keep it lively. Will you come?" Karen looked so pleased and excited that Jackie nodded even though her stomach had dropped.

"I'd be happy to."

Karen gave an uncharacteristic squeal of delight and ran back to Myles, who opened his arms, collecting her in a hug that swept her off her feet.

Jackie held herself together and gave a small wave before pushing her way through the saloon's swinging doors. As soon as she did, the January Texas air bit into her. She should have worn her boots, not these ridiculous heels. Her feet were going to be frozen by the time she walked all the way back to her car, which she'd left at April's.

The light hanging above the saloon door flickered, and she knew if she looked to the right, she'd see the edge of town, as well as a glimpse of her apartment on the corner, across and one block down. To the left and many blocks away was her car. After April's hurtful words tonight, going home without her car was a much more pleasant prospect than the idea of possibly running into her friend.

Sniffing back a sudden flood of unexpected tears, Jackie hurried down the saloon's two steps as the light above the door flickered once again, then died, instantly creating deep, dark shadows across the sidewalk. Her foot struck something solid, and a dog yipped in surprise. Jackie went down hard on the concrete as she tried to avoid falling on Rusty, a dog that always hung around the saloon.

Jackie gasped as her right hand and left knee took the brunt of her tumble. She rolled onto her back, trying to breathe through the agony, a numbing, breathtaking pain. Rusty, a brown-and-white retriever of some sort, was at her side in an instant, nuzzling her cheek.

The saloon door had opened and a cowboy was silhouetted against the light. Then the door creaked shut, and suddenly Jackie was being hoisted to her feet, a muscular arm behind her back. She staggered on her heels while a man wearing spicy aftershave held her close in the darkness.

Cole Wylder.

Being in his arms felt even better than she'd imagined. To support her, he curved his arm, pulling her against him. Her palms landed against his chest, which was firm. The stuff of fantasies. She quickly twisted her wrist, jerking her torn hand away from his shirt.

"Are you okay?" he asked. "That was a hard fall."

"You saw it?" She closed her eyes as the light above the saloon door flickered back to life. That was not how she'd planned to gain Cole's attention.

Not that she wanted his attention any longer, she reminded herself. She was moving on to new pastures, with new crushes that would actually go somewhere.

But *mmm*, he felt good.

"Let's see your hand," he commanded. He slowly released her, as though unsure whether she'd stay upright without his support, then carefully cupped her hand, a frown creasing his face. "Ouch."

"It's not that bad. Really," she said quickly. She tried to step away, wincing as her jeans scraped against her injured knee. Could you break a kneecap? Or had she just bruised it beyond comprehension?

Cole caught her arms, then crouched to inspect the damage. His white shirt was bunching at his shoulders. It had black stitching above the pockets and she recognized it as one he'd had years ago. It barely fit him now, his years away having added to his muscular build. As he gently pushed back the torn fabric, he sucked air between his teeth and adjusted his cowboy hat. She knew it likely looked bad, but having a former rodeo star act as though it truly was allowed the pain to sink in even deeper.

"Can you walk?"

"Of course." She hobbled a few steps, pride forcing her to tip her chin up in defiance of the throbbing.

"You're bleeding," Cole said. He'd crossed his arms, his shirt bunching and stretching at his shoulders again. It seemed as if he might bust out of the thing. She closed her eyes, trying to fight the image of what that might look like. "You need to get cleaned up." He stretched out an arm as though about to guide her back into the saloon, but she shook her head.

She braved a glimpse at her knee in the faint glow of light. Not good. And her new jeans weren't doing great, either, the fabric over the knee ripped and already stained by blood. She didn't even want to consider the large scuff across the toe of one of her new shoes. And she certainly didn't want to go back inside and have people fuss over her.

"I live just down the block," she said, hobbling a step toward her apartment.

He straightened. "I'll walk you."

"It's fine, really." Jackie took a few more tentative steps. "You can't leave your party."

"On the contrary." He hooked an arm around her waist, as he had earlier. The move felt natural and fluid, not at all awkward like their conversations had been since his return home. "It's my party so I can do whatever I want." He flashed her one of those patented Cole Wylder devilish smiles and that fizzy feeling enveloped her.

"Fine. Miss your welcome-back party. See if I care." Her voice sounded breathless to her own ears, and she reminded herself that he was Mr. Fun and she was no longer Miss Short-Term Fling.

Cole gave her a grin that melted her insides. "You're down this way, right?" He pointed toward her building and she nodded.

"You're not sad to miss the hoopla?" she asked, after limping along beside him for a few moments.

"It's weird being the center of attention."

"You don't like it?"

"It's as if everyone only knows..." He inhaled sharply and shook his head. Jackie felt a stab of awareness that was not at all unpleasant.

"They only know the old version of you?" she suggested, inching along beside him.

He stopped moving and looked down at her. He was about four inches taller, a sexy, sexy height that made her feel extra feminine. "Yeah."

Her heart softened. "And they don't seem to want to see who you are now?"

Their eyes met and locked for several beats, and Jackie was struck by an odd feeling. It was as though they understood each other, on some plane that nobody else in town even seemed to know existed.

Cole cleared his throat and looked away.

Jackie hazarded a few more slow, limping steps. Rusty was still fussing over her, dancing around and nudging her leg with his nose.

"This your dog?" Cole asked.

"No, this is Rusty."

A shadow crossed Cole's face. It was fleeting, but telling.

"You haven't met?" she asked casually, realizing Rusty had become a fixture in Cole's absence. She guessed it must be odd to return to a town you'd always known and have a gap in its history, missing small, new things everyone else assumed you knew.

Jackie winced and leaned closer to Cole as they stepped off the curb to cut across Main Street. It was empty other than a few vehicles parked in front of The Watering Hole. "He was a stray a few years back. He started hanging out in front of the saloon, begging for day-old cheese bread. Brant was going to find him a new home as part of his animal control duties, but by then, in just a few days, Rusty had won everyone over. The bar's owners adopted him and built him a doghouse out back. He has a dish of food and water, but still loves the cheese bread best. In the summer he ducks under the swinging doors to visit all the patrons. He's become a local institution, like Bill."

"Isn't Bill an armadillo?"

"Town mascot," Jackie confirmed. She loved Sweetheart Creek and all its quirks.

She glanced at Cole to see what he thought of her story, and he smiled, his eyes shadowed under the brim of his cowboy hat. The smile was warm and satisfying, and felt like it was just for her.

As they reached the other side of the street, Cole snugged her closer, helping her take the weight off her knee as she stepped up onto the sidewalk. It was good being in his arms, and for a moment Jackie thought that maybe one day she might have something like this, just like everyone else.

* * *

Cole helped Jackie navigate the narrow staircase that led from Main Street to the apartment above the accounting office. She was leaning on him a bit more, the creaking stairs testing her hindered mobility. With her body pressed tight to his side, she smelled like strawberries. He considered carrying her, but it didn't feel right, despite his desire to bring her ever closer. He got the impression she was holding on to something vital by a very thin string tonight, and that it might break if he didn't tread carefully.

This fragility, if you could call it that, didn't compute with the Jackie he'd always known. That woman was an unstoppable ray of sunshine. Not that this version wasn't...

On the outside Jackie was still that warm, open, smiling woman who'd always made him perk up whenever she entered a room. You never knew what she'd do, but it was sure to lead to a few laughs. He and his brothers had always been a bit afraid of Jackie, fearing what might happen if she ever caught them on the playground after all that chasing.

But tonight, and actually, ever since his return, he'd noticed a hint of something-not-quite-right stalking her glowing smiles like a shadow. He'd said something to Brant, but his brother had brushed it off. Maybe she'd been like this for so long nobody had noticed?

Or maybe Cole was just wishing he wasn't the only one entertaining ghosts and pain.

They had reached the landing at the top of the stairs, with an apartment door on either side. Jackie fumbled with her keys by the door to the right, and he took them, worked the lock, then pushed open the door.

"I always wondered what these apartments looked like," he said, as she flicked on the lights. "I heard they have quite the wait list."

The space was open, warm and cheerful, and smelled like Jackie's fruity lip balm and vanilla. It was a far cry from the functional spaces he'd been staying in over the last several years. This was a home. There were thriving plants, cheerful prints on the walls, mismatched furniture that somehow all jived together, area rugs tossed willy-nilly over the old hardwood floors. He could picture it during the day, sun-soaked and bright thanks to the large windows overlooking the street.

"Home sweet home," Jackie muttered. She'd taken a step away from him, but now reached out, tugging on his shirt. "Help me to the couch." She pointed to the sitting area in front of them. A kitchen and eating nook were to the right, overlooking the street, and to the left was a wall with two doorways, likely leading to a bedroom and a bathroom.

He complied, patiently assisting her. She clung to him, the uneasiness and quiet shyness that had defined her around him since his return, gone. She was leaning heavily on him, comfortable being so close. He liked it. It hinted at something familiar, and it gave him hope, as if he'd eroded one of the many walls between him and the people he'd once known around town.

"So what other crazy animals do I need to know about in Sweetheart Creek?" he asked as he settled her on the couch, surprised to find that the fuzzy black pillow beside her was in fact a dog.

"None that I can think of other than this little beast," Jackie said, giving her pet a fond pat. The medium-size dog had corkscrew curls, so long that its eyes were hidden behind the ridiculous shaggy fur. "This is Goose." Her voice turned affectionate, and the canine wriggled across the cushions to curl up against her side.

"Has a lot changed since you left?" She winced as Cole helped elevate her leg, propping it on the coffee table in front of her. He slipped a silky red cushion under her heel.

When he summoned the courage to look at Jackie, her expression was open and curious. No apparent judgment, just welcoming acceptance. He wanted to soak it in, pull her into his arms and give her a hug.

"I was saying at Christmas that it seemed like nothing ever changed when I lived here. But it turns out all you have to do is go away for a few years. Then everything changes." He chuckled, trying to disguise the ache in his chest that had somehow made its way into his voice.

"Well, I'm still the same."

"No, you're quieter." He settled himself on the coffee table across from her. Cole knew he should return to his party, but felt like they were precariously perched on the cusp of something good, and he didn't want to disturb whatever it might turn out to be. A conversation. A connection. A sense that he wasn't alone. A shared smile. It was small, easy to overlook or dismiss, but it somehow felt... important. Like this was the place he was supposed to be right now.

"I'm not quieter!" She seemed surprised, her face scrunched into an adorable expression of protest.

"Around me you are."

She scoffed, nothing more than a soft huff riding on a cloud of disbelief, but it made him smile, anticipating what she'd say next.

"Well, that's because I have a secret crush on you, and now that you're here in the flesh it's very difficult to think and speak." She flashed that flirtatious, fun grin he loved so much. She did such a good job of putting on the facade that he almost forgot about the sadness darkening her blue, hazel-flecked eyes. "I mean, if you stay a moment longer I can't be responsible for what I might do to you."

"Most women in your position would have ripped my clothes off already," he said, playing along. "You didn't fake this fall just to get me alone, did you?"

She choked with amused disbelief. "You think you're worth this?" She held up her shredded palm and gestured to her swollen knee. "Your ego always was mighty huge, Cole." She narrowed her eyes and dropped her voice an octave, sending tingles up his spine as she batted her lashes. "I'm glad to see that hasn't changed."

He chuckled. There was something about Jackie Moorhouse that made him want to kiss her.

"Where's your first aid kit?" he asked.

"I don't have one."

"You're right. You haven't changed, despite being quieter." He sighed loudly, as though bearing a burden. "Wild and out of control, living life without a first aid kit."

She laughed. "And do you have one. Wild Wylder?"

He tensed at the old nickname. "I'm sure there's one on the ranch," he said mildly. "So I own part of one."

Jackie laughed, the sound rich and contagious. Her face lit up, reminding him of the girl she used to be. The layer of tension and worry that had been present lifted, and it was as though everything in her world had been righted again.

By him.

But still... Cole knew better. Those shadows were still there, even if he couldn't see them at the moment.

"Point me to your bathroom," he said. "We'll get you fixed up."

"You're supposed to be at your party."

He leaned forward, placing a hand on her thigh, above her uninjured knee. She froze, her breathing coming to a halt. Maybe she still had that crush on him, after all. Or maybe she wasn't immune to the tension that suddenly coiled and crackled around them. "And what kind of host would I be if I allowed one of my guests to go home alone, wounded and without care?"

Jackie rolled her eyes and crossed her arms. He frowned. They were having a moment here; couldn't she see that? Had his moves grown that rusty?

"What?" he protested, when she continued to act unimpressed. He lifted his hand from her leg, unable to stop smiling. "I'm trying to be a gentleman."

She raised her brows, amusement dancing in her eyes.

"It's new to me," he muttered, moving aside the torn denim to study her injured knee, eager to avoid meeting her gaze.

"Okay, well, in that case you're doing very well. If I were a teacher I'd give you about a B. Maybe a B minus."

"Only a B?" He looked up indignantly. "I scooped you up off the street. I escorted you home. I haven't once done anything inappropriate."

"Well, obviously you don't read your audience very well," she said, sucking in her cheeks as though fighting a smile. Her eyes were dancing again. They were losing their darkness, turning a deep shade of blue, almost indigo. It was mesmerizing, and incredibly heady knowing he'd had that effect.

He set his hat on the table beside him, and her dog stretched and groaned with contentment. Surprised, Cole felt a sting of envy.

He fiddled with his hat before slowly looking up at Jackie again. "I'll admit I'm confused about what it takes to be a gentleman."

She was a flirt, and he knew enough to be aware that her hints to do something inappropriate weren't genuine invitations.

Not that he'd take them. He'd spent many hours sitting in a brew pub in the small mountain town of Blueberry Springs, sipping whiskey and considering the various ways he could make things right again once he returned home. If he ever did.

One of the possible solutions was to focus on his family. Another was to swear off women for a while, to give himself time to mend his reputation, instead of slipping back into his old life and reinforcing old images of himself.

He'd already spent several years alone, moving from job to job across the country to keep himself distracted from his homesickness. So another six months—long enough to prove to the town that he was a stable adult, no longer prone to making the impulsive errors of youth—wouldn't kill him.

There was also the minor fact that he wasn't much of a catch at the moment. His childhood bedroom had been turned into an office during his absence, and he was currently crashing in one brother's old bedroom on the family ranch—an operation that was profitable because of his eldest brother's hard work. Not his own. Levi had been the one to stay, take care of family, pick up and hold all the pieces Cole had left scattered when he'd left. Now that he'd returned, he didn't feel he could simply waltz in and claim his share. He had to earn it back, along with his family's trust.

In other words, he had little to provide right now. And being thirty-three, he needed to have something to offer. A house. A real stake in the family ranch. Something more than nothing.

Hence no women, even if Jackie flirted outrageously and had the most kissable, moist lips he'd seen in eons.

Realizing he was staring, he leaped from his spot on her coffee table and strode toward the back of the apartment, pausing in what turned out to be the bathroom doorway. The array of beauty products cluttered on the vanity amazed him.

This woman couldn't pack her life into a duffel bag and be on the road in fifteen minutes or less, that was for sure. He opened the medicine cabinet, flicking through the contents until he located a box of bandages. Next he found a stack of facecloths on the small rack above the toilet. He dampened one of the cloths and headed back to where his patient was waiting.

Jackie was wriggling out of her jeans, a flash of white thigh burning an image into his brain.

He pivoted, turning his back to the room, his breathing ragged.

"Sorry, I can't access my knee." He could hear her struggling with the denim and his mind roamed, imagining the full expanse of bare thighs, calves and ankles, the style and color of her underwear.

His resolve to forgo women was dissolving like tissue paper in a rainstorm. It had been a very long time indeed, and another six months felt like self-imposed torture.

"Can you help?" she asked, frustration thickening her voice.

Cole swallowed hard. "I have a feeling you're not decent..."

"Well, a lot of my jokes aren't, but at the moment I have my jacket covering anything interesting. So if you don't mind being a gentleman and tugging the cuffs of my jeans, that would be great."

"If stripping you means being a gentleman, then I might just have this in the bag," he joked, reining in his libido as he headed to the couch. Her dog had abandoned his spot and was now stretched out on an area rug near the door, belly to the sky.

Jackie's jacket was draped over her lap, and Cole struggled with the sting of disappointment upon missing a glimpse of her underwear.

"Tug here?" he asked, hooking his thumbs in the tight ankles of her jeans. "Ever heard of boot cut?"

"I was trying something new," she said, gesturing to the high heels she'd kicked under the table.

"Sexy," he said, before realizing the comment might make her uncomfortable, seeing as he was currently peeling off her jeans, and trying—and likely failing—to act as though it didn't affect him.

"That was the idea," Jackie murmured, scowling at the pink shoes.

"Catch anyone while out trolling?" he asked idly, sliding the pants from her legs. She hissed as the material grazed her left knee. He reminded himself of his personal vow to remain single. He tended to take charge of women's problems like they were his own, which had been unappreciated and a source of constant tension with April. He hurt people, and he hadn't quite figured out how not to do that yet.

There was no way he was going to take a lovely, lighthearted woman like Jackie Moorhouse and run her through the Cole wringer. Or as Brant had once called him, the human hurricane. She might look tough, but he sensed there was something delicate about her.

He gently cupped a hand over the skin above her knee. It was warm, the joint already swelling. It wouldn't be long until it was all colors of the rainbow. "Think you broke anything?"

"Hope not."

"Have any ice?"

She nodded and gestured to the kitchen.

"Here, work on cleaning up." Cole handed her the items he'd collected from the bathroom, then returned moments later with a bag of ice from her fridge freezer. He settled himself across from her once again, sitting on the table, then helped her stretch her injured leg along his thigh. Awareness prickled everywhere their bodies touched.

"Try this." He gingerly lowered the ice onto her knee. For a moment their hands connected as they positioned it. He dragged his away, wondering why the touch had felt meaningful and tender.

"Remember when you used to chase me at recess?" he asked.

"You never let me catch you," she replied, a slight scolding tone in her voice.

"What would've happened if you had?" He figured she'd been all about the pursuit. But a part of him was curious if she'd had plans for him if she'd ever managed to snag him.

"Wouldn't you like to know?" Her sly smile sent tingles up his spine again, and caused a tightness in his torso.

"I would." Their eyes locked. "And it seems as though you've currently caught me."

Her eyes, still that crazy indigo, hid behind lowered lashes for a long moment. Then she looked up, her steady gaze locked on his once again.

"Cole," she said gently, and he tensed himself for the letdown. "You're a catch-and-release cowboy."

He nodded, thinking that for the first time in a long while, he wanted to be catch-and-keep.

* * *

"What if you kept me for a spell?" Cole asked. While he'd posed the question lightly, making it easy to laugh off, Jackie's stomach filled with heat. It was an offer. An offer from Cole Wylder.

But it was for something akin to a fling. Nothing more.

"Yeah?" she asked softly, playing along, while her heart sank and her hope soared like a traitor. "How long should I keep you?"

His lake-blue eyes darkened and his tongue rolled across his top lip as though he was imagining a flavor. As though imagining kissing her?

She wriggled to the edge of the couch, her head spinning. She reached forward, allowing her good hand to drift across the shoulders she'd dreamed about for so long.

She didn't want a fling, but she could enjoy a kiss before

releasing him and the ancient crush that no longer served her, discard it like a hermit crab would its outgrown shell.

She watched him as she moved into his space. He hesitated for almost too long, then his hand slipped up her bare thigh, the other cupping her face, causing her to shiver.

When he was a breath away, he stated, "I've sworn off women."

Jackie froze. He was finally about to kiss her, and he'd sworn off women? He'd asked her to keep him, but he didn't want her?

She sighed, the sound one of longing. Cole Wylder was still destined to dart in and out of the lives of women.

And yet there was pain and regret in his hesitant confession she didn't fully understand. But she realized he was no longer the wild cowboy some folks seemed to think he was—if he ever had been.

"Me, too. I mean, I've sworn off men." Jackie's hands were on his upper thighs, holding on as though she was afraid to let go, afraid she'd listen to herself and walk away. "Flings. One-night stands. They're all a no."

She was about to lean back, break the connection, but Cole tenderly stroked her cheek, wrapping a spell around her. He was taking her in with that studious look of his, making her feel as though he was here, totally present.

"So we are both saying no."

"We are both saying no," she confirmed, hating her own lack of resistance, the way she was leaning closer, allowing the spell to weave and tighten around her like a climbing vine.

"I told myself I was going to do things differently this time," he said, after clearing his throat. He had eased back as though someone had flooded him in light, making him aware of what he'd been doing. "I have fences to mend. I'm sorry."

"I rejected you first," she said, suddenly angry with the push-pull between them, and the way he was making it seem as though she didn't understand that this wasn't going to work out.

He laughed. "I know."

"You're a tease."

"So are you," he retorted quickly.

"No, I'm a *flirt*."

"No, you tease with those pained, sad eyes, hiding behind your sunshine and laughter."

"I'm fine," she insisted, but she felt her chin tremble. Somehow, having her pain recognized made it hurt all the more.

They were quiet for a moment, Cole focused on the ice pack resting on her knee. They were still close, and he tipped forward so he could rest his forehead against hers with a sigh. Her lips were a whisper from his, and there was an urgency in his voice as he asked, "Can I kiss you anyway?"

She glanced upward, then caught her breath. He was so close. She didn't think she'd ever looked anyone in the eye at such proximity. His irises had a dark ring around the edges, and his lashes were black, intensifying the blue.

A kiss... A kiss wasn't a fling. Surely that would be okay? Something for her to carry with her like a souvenir of her long-standing, now-expired crush.

"Yes."

Finally, his lips met hers, in a kiss she'd been imagining since elementary school. The fantasy had evolved over the years from a stolen peck to one full of passion and heat. The real Cole was no disappointment.

At first the kiss was tentative and she groaned in frustration. She swept her tongue against his closed lips, wanting more. If she was relenting and kissing him, she wanted nothing held back.

His intake of breath stirred the air around them, a split second of hesitation where she sensed he'd allowed his mind to assess the situation and decide his next move. She shifted forward, sliding from the couch onto his lap, bracing herself with her good leg so she wouldn't land on the floor.

She could feel the moment Cole stopped thinking, his kisses

becoming unbridled. She could barely breathe, inhaling through her nose as she came up for air, before diving in for more. His mouth was exploratory, hungry, his response impelled by a need that matched her own.

Waves of electricity zipped between them, sharp, biting, almost painful. And filled with so much longing it took what was left of her breath away.

And in that moment Jackie knew she'd made a grave error.

One kiss with Cole was not harmless. Not by a long shot.

She pushed him away, her heart pounding. If he stayed one minute longer, she'd do the exact thing she'd promised herself she wouldn't. She'd undo everything and be that woman April had scorned and laughed at earlier in the evening. The woman who would never find love.

Jackie looked up, determined. "That was nice. But it was a mistake."

She slid back to the couch, to the safety of not being in his arms.

Cole seemed dazed, confused.

"This isn't good for either of us." She pointed to the door, unable to meet his eyes. "I'm sorry, but you need to leave."

2

Today

Cole Wylder sequestered himself in a corner of the Sweetheart Creek community barn, dutifully allowing the music and celebration of Brant and April's marriage to weave around him. He couldn't figure out the tradition of holding a wedding reception for people who eloped. Wasn't the point of eloping to avoid the whole dog and pony show?

Still, it was a Sweetheart Creek ritual to hold a reception a month after a couple made their way into Mr. Lovely's chapel for a quick elopement on New Year's Eve, and his brother's was no exception.

Cole swiped a hand over his jaw, trying to steady himself. He'd been on edge, uncomfortable in his own skin since the moment Jackie had kicked him out of her place last night. He'd walked home—several miles along darkened gravel roads—needing the space to think, having more than enough energy to burn after that kiss.

It had been just a kiss.

One kiss.

Okay, several.

And he was coming undone like a chicken locked in a henhouse with a pack of foxes.

For whatever reason, he couldn't stop thinking about Jackie.

Or the way she'd kicked him out.

She'd proclaimed he was no good for her. And that had been like a giant flashing billboard reminding him why he'd sworn off women.

Cole nodded to Travis Nestner, the town's mayor, as the man went by, clutching a cluster of plastic juice cups in his fingers, no doubt for his triplet daughters. A few paces to his left, two teenagers were kissing, and Cole swiveled, putting his back to them. The converted barn, now a community center, was where he guessed at least half the townsfolk had received their first kiss. Himself included.

And right now, seeing others lock lips only made him wonder how to get the strawberry-scented woman named Jackie Moorhouse to kiss him again.

Seriously, though. What was wrong with him? Why couldn't he think of something other than Jackie? Was it because he'd felt a connection with her that had been like a floodlight aimed at his soul when they'd touched?

It was a good thing she was stronger than he was. She was making them stick to the promises they'd expressed.

She was also right in demanding more than a night or two—which was all he was offering. Except he wasn't actually offering, was he? Because if he was, that would reflect poorly on him. And right now he was avoiding all potential negative press.

Or at least trying to.

So what had he been offering Jackie when he'd asked if he could kiss her?

Nothing. It had been purely selfish.

Which meant he hadn't changed as much as he'd hoped he had. And that meant he needed to avoid her, since she was an obvious temptation, a distraction, a hint at what could become his fresh new downfall.

He sighed as he crossed his arms, frowning at his own weakness.

"Too bad she's taken now, huh?" Wade Ross asked, leaning against the wall beside Cole. The man smelled of beer and broken dreams.

"Sorry?" Cole immediately scanned the room for Jackie before following the man's gaze to the bride. "Oh, April." Right. It was her party, last night's fight with Brant long forgotten by the looks of things. She was beaming, her arms wrapped around Cole's brother as they danced. "I'm glad they found each other."

"That's what you're supposed to say when you come back too late and lose out." The man belched and staggered off.

Cole shook his head and wondered if trying to rebuild his reputation would be an effort in futility.

"It'll take time," a woman said from beside him.

Cole turned to find Daisy-Mae Ray batting her heavily mascaraed eyelashes at him. Behind her, someone crossed the room, waving merrily at people, a bounce in her step that sported a slight limp after last night's tumble: Jackie.

Daisy-Mae was smiling up at him, not willing to accept his rejection, apparently. Maybe what Jackie had said last night hadn't been right. It wasn't that people just remembered who he'd been. Maybe they saw the real him. The one he'd tried to run from. If so, it was pointless to overwrite that version of himself, because it would always pop right back up again.

If that was the case, then Jackie was the evidence. Because despite his attempts at change, he was ready to throw it all away for a chance to be with her. He would have taken her to bed last night if she hadn't shown him the door.

He rubbed the heel of his hand over the tight spot in his chest. The dismissal still hurt.

It had just been a kiss.

And boy, had they kissed. It had been hotter than the lava that had chased him while guiding hikers down a Hawaiian volcano.

As Daisy-Mae pressed closer, whispering something in his ear, his gaze caught on a pair of sparkling eyes across the room—eyes that quickly looked away. Jackie's.

He sighed and dragged a hand over his jaw again, fighting the instinct to go to her. It was going to take a while to stop thinking about her and last night.

Maybe it really had been a mistake to kiss her, because it sure hadn't answered any of his questions about whatever it was she was hiding from the world. Instead, it had only created more.

Daisy-Mae laughed, having no doubt read how tortured he was about Jackie. "Go get her," she whispered, then winked over her shoulder as she sashayed away.

He let out a breath and turned, only to find Violet Granger facing him, a plastic glass of punch extended his way.

"Whoa!" he said, stopping short of being splashed with the orange drink. "Almost ran you over."

"Would you like one?" She waved her plastic cup of juice in front of him, her eyes bright and hopeful.

"No, thanks."

The only thing he wanted was to clear away whatever caused Jackie the sadness he saw in her eyes—even though he figured she was perfectly capable of doing it herself.

Wow. He really needed to get that woman out of his mind.

"This is quite the party, isn't it?" Violet said. She shifted so she was standing beside him, her arm pressing against his. "So tell me about your adventures." She leaned a little closer and curled the fingers of her free hand around his biceps. "I hear you were away for a few years."

She was sweet, she really was. He gently peeled her fingers from his arm. "Sorry, hon. I'm, uh…"

He didn't know how to get out of this smoothly. Violet's expression was already crumbling. It was ridiculous, but all he could think of was how Jackie might feel about him having another woman flirt with him.

No, it wasn't about Jackie. It was about turning over a new leaf, wasn't it? About making it clear to the town that he'd returned for his family and that they were his priority.

Across the building, Jackie was chatting with people, moving among the crowd gathered at the edge of the dance floor. Was she leaving? They hadn't even said hello.

No, she was doing a slow loop of the room and soon might cross his path.

Violet quirked her lips in resignation. "I heard she's been waiting for you since you left."

Cole gave himself a shake, trying to focus. "What's that?"

"Jackie."

"Pretty sure she hasn't."

She'd called kissing him a mistake, had she not?

He spun away when Violet reached for him again, and bumped into someone who'd come up behind him. His arms instinctively went around the woman, keeping her from tumbling backward. She felt familiar, safe, and a stir of longing swirled within him.

Jackie.

He was momentarily rendered speechless as their eyes connected, her fingers gripping the front of his shirt as if they'd just broken a hot, steamy kiss and she craved more. Her lower lip was red from being chewed, and he found it impossible to break his gaze.

"I thought we weren't doing this any longer," she said, amusement in her breathy voice. She hadn't loosened her grip, and her body was taut in his embrace. His hands had started their own exploring, edging from her narrow waist to her shoulder blades as if he was preparing to brace her for the demanding kiss his heart was pounding for.

He abruptly loosened his grip and shuffled backward, putting space between them. "Sorry," he said, unable to keep from eyeing her outfit's tucks and curves. She was wearing cowboy boots. Jeans that hugged her thighs like a bull rider waiting to leave the gate. A black Western shirt with pearly snaps up the front, and delicate white stitching detail that spread over the shoulders and down to where she'd left the top two snaps open. His gaze arrested, he didn't notice what she'd done with her hair.

"I'm not sorry," she whispered.

He blinked, forcing himself to break the connection. She gave him a flirtatious wink and walked away.

She was leaving him wanting once again.

It was a marvelous view, though, the Wranglers enhancing the curves of her hips and high waist. He wondered what color her underwear was tonight, and if he'd ever get a chance to see it.

Cole gave himself a shake. Wow. He really needed to get out of her orbit before he roared back into his old ways, wild and without a thought to consequences.

She'd warned him she was a flirt. This was a game that meant nothing to her. She didn't want *him*.

But he wanted her. He wanted to call out and ask how her knee was. Kiss her again. Hold her.

He lost sight of her in the thick crowd, then moments later she reappeared off to the side, near the gift table by the doors. As she circulated she would often reach out, touching someone's arm, offering a quick word and a laugh. Everyone adored her. Lots of men's gazes trailed after her.

Cole struggled with a rush of adrenaline and an urge to fight, protect and start staking claims.

Jackie, now wearing her coat near the exit, glanced over her shoulder, giving him a private smile. It hit him like a cow butting her head into his solar plexus. He needed to be close to Jackie. Now.

He lifted a foot to start after her when a small voice inside his head warned, "Don't do it. This isn't why you came home."

Cole halted in his tracks. Sure, he felt a primal urge to rest a hand on Jackie's hip and tell all the other men in the room she was his. But that was no excuse to repeat past mistakes. Just because he wanted to find out what was going on in that beautiful, cheerful woman's mind... No excuse. She deserved better, and he was moving on, changing his life.

Starting right now.

* * *

Jackie stood outside the barn, gulping a blast of frosty January air. What on earth kind of game was she playing?

She'd been jealous of Daisy-Mae, and then Violet, for flirting with Cole, and she had no right to be. One kiss did not mean a thing to a man like Cole Wylder, and she'd be wise to remember that.

Plus she had *rejected* him.

He wasn't looking to start a family or even date right now, so it didn't matter what she'd felt when they'd kissed last night, or when he'd turned around and bumped into her minutes ago. She could practically still feel the burn of his hands on her body. The way their eyes had locked, the way she'd become all too aware of everything to do with the handsome man.

The kiss had been a mistake.

Cole Wylder was not a keeper.

Jackie leaned against the cold wooden barn, undecided on what to do. Should she stay out here a bit longer to collect herself, then go back inside and dance and pretend she was loving the reception for Brant and April? Or should she leave?

If she went home, she could curl up with her tablet and binge read on the couch, with Goose nestled beside her. If she went inside the barn she could get another slice of Maria's apple pie, which was pretty darn good, too.

But going inside could lead her toward another poor decision. Another kiss. Another step into something that would surely be unhealthy.

Home it was.

JackieLynn Moorhouse was done drooling over Cole Wylder.

Again.

* * *

Cole stepped out from under the glow of the entrance light, allowing his eyes to adjust to the semidarkness. He scanned the grassy parking area behind the barn, scarcely noticing the music wafting through the night air. Almost immediately, he spotted a figure moving through the shadows.

He cupped his hands around his mouth and shouted, "Jackie!"

She spun around, and he could've sworn her face lit up before she schooled her expression. Then again, it was pretty dark, and his mind could be playing tricks on him.

It still zinged him, thinking how she'd brushed him off as a mistake. And somehow intrigued him, because how could she not have felt what he did every time they touched?

He hustled forward, weaving between rows of dusty pickup trucks, until he caught up with her.

Her eyebrows rose in question.

Shoot. He'd jumped into action without a plan. He'd stepped out for a breath of air, spied her familiar form moving across the parking lot, and had reacted.

He pushed back his hat, exposing his forehead to the chilly night, then readjusted it as though that could buy him time to think. "You leaving?"

She nodded, shifting her car keys to her other hand. "Why?

Wanna come with me?" Her tone was flirty, not serious.

He wanted to accept, but was fairly certain she was only toying with him.

He leaned against the blue Ford beside him, scratching the back of his left calf with the toe of his right boot.

"You know I do," he replied easily, pleased that his voice sounded casual.

"*Do* I know that?" she retorted smoothly.

He wasn't used to her quick responses or the fact that she seemed to be made of Teflon. Everything ended up back in his court when they bantered. She wasn't playing hard to get; she might actually *be* hard to get—despite the rumors saying she wanted him.

He'd seen Jackie Moorhouse in action, and she could take or leave Cole Wylder, her catch-and-release cowboy.

Silence stretched between them, and she didn't move toward her car with the taped-up bumper, expecting him to follow, accepting her invitation. Which meant it hadn't truly been one.

"So, uh, you regret kissing me, huh?" Cole said finally, wincing.

Not cool, man. Not cool.

To his surprise, Jackie stepped up to him, wrapped her arms around his waist and placed an ear against his chest. She snuggled in, her warmth a reprieve from the late January chill. He hadn't grabbed a jacket when he'd left the barn, and after a second's hesitation, he slid his palms across her back. Down over her ribs, the narrowing of her waist, before the flare of her hips. He stilled his hands, knowing he would have no resistance if he continued exploring. He'd kiss her again.

She'd tell him it was a mistake.

He'd feel that same hollow sense of loss once more.

"The stars are out tonight," she said.

Cole tipped his head back until the brim of his hat no longer shielded his view. Lots of stars were twinkling up there, so bright and close in the crisp night air he felt as though he could reach out and touch them.

"What are we doing?" he asked, when the silence grew once again. He was used to female contact going somewhere. Not that he was complaining. This was nice, too.

"It's called snuggling."

"Oh..." he said, drawing out the word as though comprehension was dawning. "This is what women are always wanting after sex. A body hug."

She giggled, the sound easing any lingering tension as it vibrated against him.

"*Are* you going to kiss me?" he asked, unable to help himself.

She studied him, her lips twisted in contemplation. "I haven't decided yet," she said at long last.

Amusement tugged at him. "Why not?"

"It's not you, it's me."

"Ouch." He released her, clutching at his chest as if she'd stabbed him.

She didn't laugh, and he wanted to touch her, console her, reassure and comfort her.

"We're both trying to get somewhere and..."

"And?"

"Something casual would be bad news for both of us," she said quickly. "I'm looking for more than that, and you're looking to repair your image around town. A one-nighter with the town flirt won't help."

A trace of anger had thickened her voice, as though she was as dissatisfied with her image as he was with his own.

"That's not you, Jackie. You're more than that."

She gave a short laugh that sounded pained. "Spare me, Cole. My longest relationships can't outlast a dairy product's best-before date."

"Yeah, but you have a..." He caught himself reaching for her, and dropped his hand. He didn't have the words to heal her.

"I have a what?" she asked. The anger was gone, and he swore a sadness and need to be recognized had replaced it.

She seemed so alone.

He shook his head, knowing he was projecting again.

"You have a sadness," he said, looking away. At the truck beside him, the dry grass underfoot, the stars shining brightly in the sky. Anywhere but at her.

It felt important to connect with this woman, to tap into that pain so it could be released. But he didn't know how to get from here to there. And even if he tried to, he had a feeling Jackie might put up barricades.

Anyway, something like that would lead to entanglements, which would distract him from working on his family relationships.

"You have a sadness, too," she replied at long last.

He finally allowed his glance to skitter her way. "I do?"

"Yes. You're different than you were."

They regarded each other for a moment.

"Are you okay?" he asked.

"Me?" She laughed, the heaviness that had settled over them broken like a flock of birds startled out of a bush. "I'm fine. It's you I'm worried about."

"Jackie," he whispered, sliding one hand around her waist and tipping her chin up with the other. "Have I ever told you you're an amazing liar?"

* * *

"Excuse me?" Had Cole just called her a liar?

"You're doing as okay as I am," Cole murmured, his voice low and deep. He still had her chin propped on his pointer finger, his body close to hers. They really had to stop meeting this way. "And the kiss wasn't a mistake."

"It wasn't?"

"It was the highlight of my year."

"We've barely finished January." She ignored the thrill she felt at the idea that Cole had enjoyed kissing her. It had felt pretty spectacular from her side of things, but she had the benefit of years of crushing on the man.

She needed to tread carefully, or she was going to fall for Cole. For real. More than some silly little crush.

"Fine, then. The highlight of the past twelve months. And the year before." He released her chin. "For a very, very long time. I only wish our timing was better."

"Right!" she agreed, giving him a wry look that loosened any tension that had built up, putting them back on track. Just friends. Light and fun. Not talking about things that could impact her fluttering, failing heart.

"If I was in a place where I was looking for something serious..." Cole paused again, as though afraid to misstep. But he was also acting as though she was some desperate, clinging woman he had to let down carefully so she didn't go berserk. Wasn't she the woman who'd shown him the door last night?

"Why do you assume I want the bother of a boyfriend and someone who's around all the time?" She flicked the brim of his hat, then crossed her arms, jutting out a hip.

"Don't you?" he asked, tugging his hat back into place.

Automatically, her gaze cut to the side, revealing the truth before she could lie to him. Nuts. What was it about this man that made her constantly tip her hand?

"Then I'd better give you a goodbye kiss," Cole whispered.

"What?" Jackie felt her heart beat faster.

"Kiss you goodbye so you can go about your life."

She smiled, knowing it was a line, but adoring it for what it was. A move to get what he wanted.

"You're such a player," she said coyly.

He stepped back as though hurt. She reached out, grabbed his shoulders and pulled him close. Their lips locked within seconds, and Jackie draped her arms around Cole's neck. His body felt so good snugged up against hers, and she dreamily wondered how long their resolve would last before they found another reason to kiss.

She caught herself. What was she doing? She was practically offering herself up as a second helping of repeated mistakes.

Although this was a goodbye kiss.

A goodbye kiss that seemed to say hello!

They finally broke apart, stirring the cold air around them. She sighed, her arms still draped across his shoulders. "Don't let it go to your head, but I've gotta tell you. Nobody can kiss like you."

She caught herself moving toward his mouth again, as though magnetized. He caught her, giving her a long, deep kiss, and she felt any lingering resolve to end it weaken.

It didn't seem to matter what she told herself. As soon as Cole's eyes met hers, or he touched her, every grain of logic and resistance fell away. And then she began to wonder… Could this work? What was the harm in what they were doing? They both knew it wasn't going anywhere real. And it wasn't like she had anything better to do with her time, or any other offers out there… Man, she was trying so hard to change, and here she was, right back to thinking like her old self, looking for trouble. No wonder she hadn't yet found love.

She pushed away. "If we go any further, someone's going to get hurt, because this is not what we want. It's not part of the plan."

"Although, if you got hurt…" He bent to the side as though he could study her knee through her jeans. It was still tender and rainbow-colored after last night's tumble over Rusty. "…maybe I could kiss you better."

"Cheesy," she warned.

"I know." He shot her a look filled with apology. "Is your knee okay?"

"It's fine. Mostly."

"I'm totally open to kissing it better." His gaze tracked downward again. "If I recall, you have very sexy legs."

She shivered at the idea of his lips on her skin. He was grinning, and heat and tension were building between them like a sudden storm that could bring a flash flood. She struggled against the pull of temptation; the gravity drawing her into the black hole of kissing him again.

"I'm pretty sure this whole thing is a bad idea," she stated. With a sharp inhale to brace herself, she stepped back, hitting the fob to unlock her car. A shooting star glided across the dark night. She didn't have time to make a wish before it was gone.

"I'm sorry. I…" She was facing him again, and could feel herself leaning closer, waiting for one of them to break, to lead them into another kiss. She needed to leave. Now.

"It's fine," Cole said quickly, shoving a hand into his hair after pulling off his hat. Then he took a large step forward, dropping his hat back on his head. "You drive me crazy, you know that?" He pulled her in for a kiss that was long, hard and deep.

She gasped for air when he ended it, dizzy with the knowledge that she had this effect on him.

"Totally crazy." He forced himself to step back, and she knew he wasn't being a player. This wasn't an act to get what he wanted. It wasn't a line.

It was the truth.

Dangerous, dangerous truth.

"You drive me crazy, too," she admitted.

"Promise me." He cleared his throat.

"Promise what?"

"That you'll be the strong one."

"The strong one?"

"Because you make it difficult to say no." As though realizing what he'd said, he chuckled, all awkward and boyish. She hated how it endeared him to her all the more.

She'd naively believed that Cole returning to Sweetheart Creek as a changed man would save her from her crush. So far it had made her only more intrigued, and him even more irresistible.

Cole's bright eyes locked on hers, and she felt that gallop her heart did whenever it seemed as though he saw only her. He brushed a strand of hair off her face.

"You know I won't be able to think of anything other than when I'll get to kiss you again," she said in a husky voice. Jackie batted her lashes, masking the truth. She *wouldn't* be able to stop thinking about kissing him again, but he didn't need to know that.

He laughed, his eyes crinkling, before he grew serious again. "Me, too, Jackie." He gave her a soft kiss. It was tender and full of promise.

"You keep kissing me."

"That one was a goodbye."

"It was? Hmm. Barely even registered."

He choked on a laugh. "You wound me, woman."

"It's why you adore me, and won't ever stop thinking of me. Try not to turn into a stalker, m'kay?"

He was smiling, trying to fight it and losing. "You are the most spectacular woman in Sweetheart Creek, you know that?"

"I do." She winked and climbed partway into her car, breathless with the idea of being called spectacular. "But don't start thanking me yet. I plan to fully torture you."

"Yeah? How so?" He leaned against the car's frame, holding her door.

She lifted a shoulder. "I'm sure I'll think of a few ways."

"I'm certain you will."

He closed the door, and she forced herself to steer her car home before she changed her mind and threw herself all over the man who, with just a few kisses, had managed to fully capture her heart.

3

Cole wasn't sure why he'd kissed Jackie again last weekend. He also wasn't sure why he was trying so hard to do the opposite of what he used to do. And if that was the case, then based on how he used to run from Jackie, he should now be jumping into her arms, right?

But the old Cole had smashed through a lot of fences on his way out of town, and the new Cole needed to keep his undivided focus on mending them. And Jackie was a distraction.

Plus, judging by the tightening in his chest whenever he thought about keeping Jackie, the new Cole wasn't ready for something serious, and she wanted a boyfriend. Her expression had given her away, despite her claim to the contrary.

It had been days since their last kiss and he couldn't get her off his mind. It didn't help that Levi wasn't loading him up with work on the ranch, but leaving him at loose ends more often than was good for him.

"You gonna drink that coffee or just stare at it?" Mrs. Fisher asked, hustling past, her arm loaded with plates of food.

Cole was surprised the woman was still waitressing at the Longhorn Diner. She'd seemed pretty old to him when he'd been in high school. Now that he was thirty-three, he realized she hadn't actually been that old back then. But now? She was likely nearing sixty and still keeping the town fed and caffeinated like she was thirty years younger.

"Stare at it," he replied, then took a sip, finding the bitter taste comforting.

Several stools down the counter a man with a full head of white hair stood with a chuckle. He dropped more bills than were necessary on the counter for Mrs. Fisher. "That's what I do when I come in here, too." He winked at the waitress, who rolled her eyes with a weary sigh.

"Garfield, you're leaving too much money again."

"It's a tip. It's not every day a man my age gets to enjoy such a beautiful view."

Mrs. Fisher pursed her lips, but Cole noted the hint of pink that had appeared in her cheeks at the compliment.

Realizing he'd been hunched on his stool for at least twenty minutes, Cole arched back and stretched out his arms, then clasped his hands behind his neck and twisted from side to side. Years of rodeo hadn't done his body any favors, but some yoga moves he'd picked up from nature guide and yoga instructor Jen Kulak, over in Blueberry Springs, Colorado, had helped. When he remembered to do them.

"Mmm. You been working out, Cole?"

The sweet female voice had him twisting toward the stool on his left. He lowered his arms as Daisy-Mae Ray licked her lips; her gaze doing a slow crawl over his biceps and shoulders.

"What's up, Daisy-Mae?" He hunched back over his coffee, wishing he could hide. He was getting tired of the attention. There'd been a time when he'd have rolled around in it like a dog that had found something that smelled particularly appetizing.

"Not much." She crossed her arms and leaned her elbows on the counter, pressing her impressive cleavage against the V of her shirt.

Cole cleared his throat and looked the other way. A woman had slid in on his other side, as well. Myles's girlfriend, Karen Hartley, the town librarian. She was the opposite of Daisy-Mae, with her dark hair, and blouse buttoned to her collarbone. She was cute. Pretty. And oh so serious.

"The library is having an auction," she announced.

"We need bachelors," Daisy-Mae cooed, lowering her lashes and batting them twice when Cole glanced back at her.

"It's not like that." Karen had set a clipboard on the counter, pen poised above a list. "Would you help us?"

He opened his mouth to decline, but she quickly carried on. "On Friday the thirteenth"—she gave a tiny shiver—"we're having an auction as well as a wine and cheese social. Free admittance."

"Free? I didn't hear that," Mrs. Fisher said, strolling past. She paused, smoothing her half apron over her hips before picking up the full coffeepot.

"If more than fifty county residents participate we're eligible for a nice-sized grant."

"So we need to get people in the door," Daisy-Mae explained.

"We also welcome donations, but I'm sure the auction will more than cover the cost of the wine and cheese," Karen said crisply, her spine straightening as she adjusted her dark-rimmed glasses.

"People make poor decisions when they've had a few drinks," Daisy-Mae said, stroking her neck with her long, lacquered nails.

"We aren't promoting bad decisions," Karen warned her.

"It's a bachelor auction," Daisy-Mae pointed out.

Karen raised her voice, her exasperation clear. "It's not like that, Daisy-Mae. We aren't auctioning dates. This is different. And it's done blindly."

"Do you like to be blindfolded?" Daisy-Mae asked Cole, giggling. The woman was incorrigible.

He stared at the small window to the diner's kitchen. He would offer to scour that greased-up grill for free for the rest of the year if he thought it might get him out of this conversation.

"Nobody is blindfolded," Karen muttered tersely.

"You get so wound up," Daisy-Mae said playfully. She leaned over and snagged a clean cup, then flagged down Mrs. Fisher, who had moved along the counter with her coffeepot.

"You want one, Karen?" Mrs. Fisher asked, as she returned to fill Daisy-Mae's.

The librarian shook her head and smoothed a hand down the sheet on her clipboard. Cole held out his cup for Mrs. Fisher, receiving a top up.

As the waitress moved away, he realized he would have been smarter to ask for his tab so he could escape before he got roped into saving the library or some such thing.

Then again, that's what the old Cole would have done —escaped.

He was kind of missing that guy right now.

Karen adjusted her glasses again and pivoted to face him. "I don't know if you've heard, but they almost shut the library down a few months ago."

"You and Myles put on a fair, right?" He blew on his coffee, then took a tentative sip. Perfect temperature.

Karen brightened at his brother's name. She had it bad. It made Cole a bit envious. It also made him think of Jackie.

Then again, he'd spotted a shirt the same color as Jackie's eyes in the window of Jenny's shop, Blue Tumbleweed, and thought of her then, too.

"We raised a lot, but not quite enough to keep the library open for the full year." Karen looked down at her clipboard, and Cole got the feeling she wasn't planning on giving him the full story when it came to this auction.

He sipped his coffee and waited. He could make up an excuse and go, but now he was curious. Did she need him to help rope Myles into something?

"So this is a matchmaking night?" Mrs. Fisher asked, sliding a few packets of sugar to Daisy-Mae as she went past.

Cole caught Karen flashing Daisy-Mae a panicked look.

He was pretty sure that was his cue to leave.

He pushed back as though about to stand. "I'm not open for matchmaking at the moment, thanks. And I'm pretty sure none of my brothers are, either." He plucked his hat off the counter and adjusted it over his brow. "Sorry."

Before he could stand, Karen clamped a hand over his wrist. Her grip was firm."It's not like that. It's a social event and an odd-job auction."

"It's called the Sweetheart Creek Bachelor Auction," Daisy-Mae proclaimed.

"No," Karen said firmly. "It's the Valentine's Day Odd Job Auction."

"I still prefer my name," Daisy-Mae said, stirring her coffee, her spoon clinking.

"So, what is it?" Cole asked, settling back into his spot.

"People share their skills and interests when they sign up, as well as the odd job they need help with. We do some matching in the background before the event. During Friday's auction, you only get to bid—"

"Blindly!" Daisy-Mae interjected.

"—on people who fall into the category we matched you with. We do that behind the scenes, based on your questionnaire answers. So then at the auction on the thirteenth you find someone to help you with your odd job on Valentine's Day. You spend the day together working on them, have lunch, and then join the group for supper."

That didn't sound like anything he'd ever heard of.

"Did y'all come up with this?"

Karen nodded.

"But its success hinges on having enough people," Daisy-Mae said.

"So on auction day—"

"What's happening on auction day?" a white-haired man asked from the end of the counter. It was Cole's great-uncle Henry Wylder, scowling at them. "Is that brother of yours buying more no-good horses just so he can store them over at Carly Clarke's and make doe eyes at her?"

"We're going to auction you off in a matchmaking game," Karen stated primly, her pen poised over the clipboard. "Can I put you down as a yes?"

Cole swallowed a chuckle as the man jerked as though someone had jabbed his back end with a live cattle prod. Henry's scowl deepened, and he turned his shoulder, even though it meant facing the wall to his left.

Karen, looking pleased, glanced back at Cole. "As I was saying, we match people up and give them a number based on a category. So, say you were interested in helping with a carpentry project, we would match you with a certain number for that. Then whoever is looking for help with carpentry bids on it."

"That's the matchmaking part," Daisy-Mae said. "But we hide the person they're bidding on behind a curtain."

"We'd read your description, to help them bid on the right person in their category of interest."

"You don't know who you've won until the big reveal at the end." Daisy-May made a trumpeting sound and waved her hands as though displaying a prize.

"Sounds like human trafficking," Henry grumbled. "And prostitution."

Karen flushed. "It's not."

Daisy-Mae said with authority, "Miss Prim would never break the law."

"And then the *next* day," Karen said with special emphasis, "on the fourteenth—"

"That's Valentine's Day." Daisy-Mae leaned toward Cole,

nearly sloshing her coffee on the sleeve of his jacket in the process.

"—everyone meets up for their odd-job day."

"What if you don't need help with anything?"

"I'm sure you could think of something, Cole," Mrs. Fisher said. "You live on a ranch. Y'all could detail one of the trucks or brush down some horses for Betty in the riding stable."

Cole couldn't imagine paying to do that with a participant he hadn't chosen. What if he got matched with someone who just wanted to paw him all day?

"This is supposed to be fun," Karen said. "No romantic expectations. No obligation to make it a date. We're raising money for the library and creating a new social event."

"Can married people join? I have an odd-job list as long as an elephant's trunk," Mrs. Fisher stated. She caught Karen's look and hurriedly added, "Relax. My yard is a fright, is all."

"I can help you, Mrs. Fisher," Cole said, finishing his coffee.

"Don't worry, I'm sure Myles will take care of it. I'll drop a hint." She winked and went to retrieve two meals from the cook as the order-up bell rang.

"So let me get this straight," Cole turned to Karen once again. "Some poor woman blindly spends money on the opportunity to have some guy fix some stuff for her. Then she's gotta fix something for him. And they have to go on a date?"

Karen was gnawing on her bottom lip, doubt shading her formerly bright expression.

"Yes!" Daisy-Mae said. She slapped her palms on the counter, making her coffee cup jump. "And both parties pay a fee to participate. Fifty bucks."

"Fifty?" Cole scowled, feeling like his uncle.

"Yes, fifty. That's only $13.50 an hour for the help. That's a good deal."

"But that's not an auction."

"Yes it is." Her expression turned sly. "The guy issues a challenge and whatever woman can complete it wins."

"A challenge?"

"Silly stuff. Like who can carry the most library books across the room without dropping any."

That could be interesting.

"Can we put you down as a bachelor?" Karen asked.

Normally he would say no...

"A bunch of people are going," Daisy-Mae said. "Me, Jenny Oliver. And I heard Jackie saying she needs her bumper fixed from when she swerved to miss Bill on Christmas Day."

"Darn near killed her passenger," Henry grumbled. When the trio looked over, he jerked a thumb at his chest. "Me. I told her to be careful, but she didn't listen. Could have given me a heart attack."

Jackie.

Cole turned to Karen. "Do you want my fifty bucks now or later?"

* * *

Jackie accepted the glass of wine from Karen Hartley in the renovated barn just outside Sweetheart Creek. Tomorrow was Valentine's Day, and she'd signed up for the auction to support the library, and to help where she could. And maybe to be busy tomorrow.

"Grab yourself a table," Karen said, steering her to an empty one near the front.

"But don't you still need help?" She'd been at the barn after work to help with setup, and was hoping that, despite being sent home to "spruce herself up," she could continue to help out rather than be a bidder. They'd already set up a microphone near the barn's large doors and strung bedsheets from the thick wooden rafters above, to create a backstage area where the bachelors could mingle without being seen. Surely there was more to be done.

"We're good. The auction starts in two minutes. Do you have your number?" Karen consulted her clipboard and handed Jackie a red card with a four written on it with thick marker.

"My lucky number."

"We hope so," Daisy-Mae said, sashaying over and giving Karen a wink. With a flounce, she sat in one of the hard folding chairs at Jackie's table.

"Are you sure you don't need more help?" Jackie asked Karen before sitting down.

She shook her head. Myles was adjusting the sound system along with Levi, the brothers helping their girlfriends with tonight's event.

"Well, then. I guess I'd better bid on someone mechanical. Maybe I can get my bumper fixed," Jackie said, crossing her fingers.

"And find a boyfriend for tomorrow night," Daisy-Mae said, checking her reflection in a pocket mirror.

"Please let him not be ancient," Jackie joked, resolving to be a good sport even though her heart wasn't in the mood for a bachelor auction.

Daisy-Mae reached over and gave her a high five. "Amen, sister."

It felt as though most of her friends had paired up lately, which meant they hadn't been suckered into bidding on a man who might or might not turn out to be a lecherous sleazebag.

Not that Sweetheart Creek had many of those, but knowing her luck, that's who she'd end up with. She took a moment to scan the barn's occupants. There were still enough single people in town to give the bachelors a few options, but at least half the women in the audience were younger than Jackie, making her feel old. What if the men on the other side of the curtain were crossing their fingers and hoping they didn't get set up with someone like her?

She placed her number flat on the table, wondering if Karen would be upset if she didn't bid. Though her friend had insisted the auction was about getting things crossed off people's to-do lists, while socializing and raising money, Jackie knew it was a matchmaking event. And for whatever reason, she couldn't find the enthusiasm for it. Maybe it was the fact that she was looking for something a bit more serious than a good time purchased at an auction.

Jenny Oliver joined her and Daisy-Mae at the rectangular table, sliding in between them. "What number do you have?" she asked, holding up a six.

Jackie showed hers, and so did Daisy-Mae, who also had a four.

"May the best woman win," Daisy-Mae said.

"Thank goodness it's a *blind* auction." Jackie gave Daisy-Mae an appraising look, and the woman laughed. She was a former Miss Sweet Hills County beauty queen and had a way of turning men's brains into pudding with just one dazzling smile.

"I hear we have to do challenges if there's a tie," Jackie said. Thankfully. Otherwise, if based on a schoolyard pick, Jackie was fairly certain they would leave her empty-handed if she went up against Daisy-Mae.

"Apparently someone forgot to look up the definition of 'auction,'" Jenny muttered.

"Works for me. I don't have a lot of spare cash these days." Daisy-Mae tugged at her tight blouse and smoothed a few strands of hair into her up-do.

"Why not?"

Daisy-Mae shrugged off the question. She was a bit of an entrepreneur, renting out that crazy free-gravity trampoline thing Karen and Myles had borrowed for the library's fall fair.

Karen cleared her throat at the microphone and Laura Oakes,

Levi's girlfriend, a former fashion model, appeared from behind the curtain to stand beside her. The long stretch of fabric billowed behind them, drawing Jackie's attention to the occasional deep voice filtering to where she was sitting. She strained her ears to identify them and noticed Daisy-Mae doing the same.

"I wish we knew who we were bidding on," Jenny said.

"It's not fair they don't get to strut their stuff for us," Daisy-Mae added.

"You can't see the men because this is a blind match-up," Karen announced, looking at her friends in the front row. "And it's also not about matchmaking. It's about getting items off our to-do lists with help from someone in the county."

Daisy-Mae rolled her eyes. "Whatever. We all know why we're here."

The other women cheered.

"Bring on the men!" someone from the back shouted.

Jackie laughed and turned to face those seated behind her, giving them two thumbs-up.

The curtain behind Karen billowed again and the owner of the local rodeo grounds, Ranger Torrington, peeked out, scanning the crowd. When he made eye contact with someone behind Jackie, he held up two fingers and mouthed *"Two."*

So not fair.

Laura shooed Ranger back behind the curtain.

The man was cute, had inherited a ranch and the rodeo grounds at age twenty-five, and now at age twenty-seven had apparently already chosen his winner.

Matchmaking was already happening.

Jackie felt a tremor of excitement despite herself. Daisy-Mae was grinning widely, and Jenny looked pale. Daisy-Mae leaned out of her chair, her focus on the bottom of the curtain, watching for flashes of footwear.

"That's Owen Lancaster," she announced with authority. "Did you hear his family owns a huge spread east of town?"

"The Wylders' new hired hand?" Jenny asked, growing paler. "How do you know?"

"Didn't you sell him those boots?" Daisy-Mae asked, still watching the curtain's hem.

"I've sold thirteen pairs in that style since October."

"Why is he working for the Wylders?" Jackie asked.

Daisy-Mae shrugged. "I heard he had a falling out with his dad." Her face creased in concentration, then she brightened. "That's Maverick Blades! The NHL star!"

The murmur in the room grew louder as women stood, trying to see what Daisy-Mae had.

Karen appeared to be panicking. "We can't guarantee who's here or not here," Laura said, taking Karen's microphone and speaking into it. "Maybe we have some local celebrities and maybe we don't. Maybe we have someone here for you who will be your own celebrity."

"That doesn't make sense," Jenny said.

"They're freaking out because I was right," Daisy-Mae said smugly. "Did you hear he's starting his own team this year?"

"He just got traded to the new team in Houston," Jackie said, correcting her. "And how do you know what his shoes look like?"

The woman gave her a serene, knowing look. Daisy-Mae was going home with a man, and it would definitely be the one she wanted.

But who did Jackie want? And if she dared think who that man might be... was he even here?

Not likely. This wasn't Cole's scene. Not that she was looking for Cole Wylder, because that would be a big uh-oh. And even if he was here? They wouldn't be paired together. There wasn't anything to connect them to each other beyond a few hot kisses and flirty fun. And they'd both sworn off that.

"If you have a number six on your card," Karen said into the microphone, "then you have been matched up with this bachelor as a possibility, since you've both written down similar interests.

After hearing his description, simply raise your number to bid. If we have more than one bidder, then the man behind the curtain will issue a challenge. The winner gets him for tomorrow, and he gets you. Remember, nothing kinky. Just helping each other out, and a nice little lunch break in between."

"That's boring," Jenny muttered.

"Nothing kinky?" Daisy-Mae sighed and raised her eyes to the string of white lights hanging above them. "We can't help it if some hanky-panky happens." She caught Karen's glance, then languidly lifted an eyebrow. Yup. She turned men into puddles, all right, and made serious librarians blush.

"I hope some hanky-panky happens," Jenny said, with a sigh of her own. "It's been a long time."

"I'll bring you to a football game next season," Jackie promised. She'd created quite a few couples at games last year, solidifying her title as the community matchmaker.

"How many games did I attend with you?" Daisy-Mae complained. "And look at my finger." She thrust out her hand. "Still bare."

"I'll definitely get you hooked up in the coming season," Jackie promised, hoping her matchmaking prowess pulled through for her friend.

"Our first man is handy," Karen announced.

"Handsy?" Jackie called.

Karen gave her a stern look.

What? She'd said she wanted lively, fun people here. Jackie was being lively.

"Handy. He's an expert with sticky doors, broken screens and painting walls and house trim."

"Yawn," Daisy-Mae said, patting her mouth. Jenny grabbed her hand, hushing her.

"Any sixes here tonight who need a handyman?"

Daisy-Mae tried to make Jenny raise her number.

"He's looking for a woman who can cook and freeze him a

month's worth of meals," Karen read. Most of the numbers that had been raised dropped instantly.

Jackie cupped her hands and hollered, "It's called the frozen foods aisle, sweetheart. Someone needs to check the year. Women left the kitchen years ago."

Some of the women laughed and nodded.

"Ladies," Karen exclaimed, her tone almost begging, "this is a good deal. If you know how to cook, a couple hours in the kitchen will get all those pesky broken, sticky doors in your home fixed."

"That's what my landlord is for," Jackie muttered. "If I wanted that kind of nuisance, I'd own a house."

"Can I bid on this guy even though I have the wrong number?" Daisy-Mae called out.

Karen glanced at Laura, who was shuffling papers. She shrugged.

"If nobody else bids, then yes," Karen declared.

"I thought you said 'yawn'?" Jackie said to Daisy-Mae, who ignored her. "And when did you learn to cook?"

"It's called the internet."

"I'm bidding! I'm bidding! Don't open it up to other numbers," MayBeth Albright hollered. She was a library volunteer in her fifties, and as Jackie recalled, she made amazing muffins, meaning her cooking would likely satisfy any man. Plus she lived in one of the tiny original homes a block off Main Street, which was a handyman's dream.

Jackie spun in her seat. MayBeth was the last remaining bidder. She was beaming, her excitement clear.

"Oh my gosh. We have a match," Jackie said.

"You're our winning bid, MayBeth," Karen said, looking pleased. "Congratulations."

The crowd cheered as Laura pulled back the curtain's edge and a tall man with broad shoulders stepped forward. His eyes met MayBeth's and Jackie could have sworn the woman nearly swooned. He was probably five years younger, but the way the two looked at each other had promise.

Jackie sighed, her matchmaking heart satisfied. "I bet they're married in a year and a half," she whispered to Jenny, who looked at her like she was crazy.

Daisy-Mae leaned forward to speak across Jenny. "Less than a year. Have you forgotten where we live? I bet she has a ring on her finger in five months or less."

"We weren't talking about a ring, we're talking about a wedding. MayBeth has a large family, and it's going to take a lot to plan her big event. Year and a half."

Daisy-Mae shrugged, then agreed. "Ring in five months or less, wedding in less than a year and a half."

"You're both incorrigible," Jenny said. She brightened. "Do me! How long for me?"

"You have to find someone first."

"Just like the rest of us," Daisy-Mae declared.

Jackie nodded, suddenly very aware that she had already found someone. Someone who would never work out. Maybe she should really get into this auction tonight and go crazy with some bids. Maybe that's all it would take to meet someone new. Someone who would distract her from thinking about Cole all the time.

"Our next helpful bachelor is a four," Karen announced, consulting her clipboard. "Ladies, if you have number four, listen up!"

Daisy-Mae and Jackie both straightened in their chairs, not daring to look at each other.

The audience was growing louder, the power of wine and a win for MayBeth under their belts.

"This man is handy, strong and a jack-of-all-trades. He's looking for a woman who doesn't mind his scattered skills and a little teasing during their workday. He says he's someone you can rely on."

Karen's gaze met Jackie's before darting away.

She was matchmaking for her? That was so sweet. Jackie could use someone to get her mind off Cole Wylder.

And this jack-of-all-trades sounded like someone who might fix her car.

Jackie raised her red card. "I'm in!"

* * *

Cole could hear laughter and loud chatter on the other side of the curtain, but he couldn't make out what Karen was saying. The speakers pointed out into the crowd rather than toward where he was standing, surrounded by idly chatting men. He hoped he'd be called early in the auction, before the women got too crazy.

"What did you get me into?" Owen Lancaster, the Sweet Meadows Ranch's newest hired hand, asked him as someone let out a wine-fueled whoop.

"No idea," Cole commented with a grimace. The laughter on the other side of the white curtain was sounding like something the old Cole would have thrived on. It was a good thing he was a community-minded man now. Although putting himself out there like a piece of meat to be auctioned off, and fought over by the crazed women of Sweetheart Creek, probably wasn't a move in the right direction. Even if it was to help the library.

And maybe get paired up with Jackie.

There. She'd wormed her way into his thoughts again, hadn't she? But maybe she could be a perfect match—non-romantically—in this auction. Someone fun to brighten his day, but not interested in anything other than friendship. They could work together tomorrow and then go their separate ways.

Smiling to himself, he realized Laura was trying to get his attention.

"Sorry, what?"

"You're up." She had come around the corner of the curtain.

"Me?"

"You. Number four. And we're going to need a challenge."

What was she talking about?

"We have eight ladies who found your description appealing." Her smile made him sick to his stomach.

Eight?

"The good news," she said, hugging her clipboard, "is that you only end up with one."

"Eight," Owen said with a chuckle, elbowing Cole in the ribs. "What did you write in your description?"

"What did you say in yours? You like long horseback rides and home-cooked meals?"

Owen turned the color of the sheet hanging beside them.

"You did, didn't you?"

"No." The man looked away.

"You know, you could have raised a lot more money if you'd put this guy on the poster and then asked those ladies to pull out their wallets." Cole pointed to Maverick Blades, a family friend who played in the NHL.

"Or…" Cole turned to Owen "…mentioned we have a former Mr. MLB Rookie of the Year."

"That was a long time ago," he muttered.

Two years ago, according to local gossip. And yet the man was hiding out in Sweetheart Creek. One day Cole would have to get the story from him.

"We need a challenge," Laura repeated, her tone urgent.

"I don't know what you mean," Cole replied.

"Didn't you read the sheet Karen gave you?"

Cole glanced at the other men, who all shrugged.

Laura rolled her eyes, then stepped closer, her blue cowboy boots helping her to match his height as well as that of several other of the bachelors.

"When we have more than one woman bidding on a candidate, we issue a challenge. The bidders face off, and the winner is paired with you."

"I like the sound of this," Maverick said with a rugged grin. He hadn't shaved today, and the five o'clock shadow contouring his jaw made him look like a hunk any woman with a heartbeat would desire. Karen could have cleaned out the Sweetheart Creek Credit Union if she'd advertised him.

"Find a razor," Cole retorted.

Maverick smirked and stroked his bristly chin.

"Ideally, your challenge speaks to who you are," Laura said. "You know, thin the herd."

"Best joke. That's my challenge," Owen said, crossing his arms and tipping back in his cowboy boots. He pointed both fingers at Laura. "You got it? That one's all mine." He gave Cole a narrow-eyed look as though daring him to steal the idea.

"Who says you're going to need one?" Cole asked.

"You did." Owen looked smug. He was a quiet guy, but once you got to know him… man, he was a pain in the butt. Fun, though.

"Thank you," Laura said smoothly to Owen, making a note on her clipboard. "I like a helpful man who can think on his feet." She turned her attention back to Cole, all focused and Zen. And maybe not entirely impressed with him at the moment.

Wasn't that something he was supposed to be working on? Being a good, helpful guy who didn't make life difficult for those around him?

On the other side of the curtain, a chant had started up: *Challenge! Challenge!*

"The women are waiting," Owen prompted.

Sweat prickled Cole's spine. He said the first thing that popped into his head. "Arm wrestle."

Laura watched him for a beat, then headed to the other side of the curtain.

Cole sucked air through his teeth and winced at the lameness of his challenge. Those were women out there, not men.

Owen laughed and slapped him on the back. "Why didn't you just suggest mud wrestling?"

Cole scowled and crossed his arms. Reinventing himself was difficult. He should have thought of something witty and yet sensitive. Not a wrestling match.

Then again, with a wrestling match, he'd be less likely to win a woman who'd spend the day making eyes at him. She'd hog-tie him and toss him in the back of his truck instead. He shuddered as Karen announced the challenge.

Naturally, she received plenty of groans. He was ready to scratch his name from the list and go home when he heard her voice.

Jackie. She was here.

And she had bid on his number—on him.

Suddenly, despite his vow to focus on nothing but family for the next several months, he wished he'd chosen a challenge so specific that only Jackie Moorhouse could win.

* * *

"Arm wrestle?" Jackie crowed. Okay, this whole auction thing had just got a lot more fun. And now she was even more intrigued about the man behind the curtain.

"What kind of brute are we bidding for?" Daisy-Mae asked, her lip curled in disgust.

Jackie sized up the women who had bid on the bachelor. She wasn't the strongest, but two contenders had already tossed their cards facedown on the table, bowing out. At the very least she could help Karen keep things fun, even if she didn't win this particular man.

"You can't change your mind!" Laura was scolding the man behind the curtain. "It's been announced." She lowered her voice, but the microphone still picked up what she said next. "And no, I'm not asking them to guess your middle name."

"Bronson! William! Mack!" Jackie hollered. "Joseph. George?"

Laura gave her a dark look.

"He doesn't have one!" Jackie dissolved into giggles.

"Oh my." Daisy-Mae reached over and removed Jackie's glass of wine. "Let's cut you off now so you don't wind up making the front page of the paper, 'kay?"

"Ladies, come on up here," Karen said. "We'll have three separate arm wrestling competitions. The winners will advance to a second challenge."

Jackie edged away from Matty, a woman who ran her own ranch and had forearms as beefy as Jackie's calves. If she was going to be paired up, she wanted it to be with someone like Violet Granger, whose version of arm exercises was answering the phone for the mayor, part of her job as his administrative assistant.

The first two contenders went head-to-head, with Matty winning. She jumped up and let out a triumphant holler, and the loser snagged a second glass of wine on her way back to her table.

"Jackie and Daisy-Mae," Karen said, moving them to one side. "You'll go third. Violet and Anna, you're next."

While the second contest began, Laura and Karen bent their heads together, murmuring. The chants, hoots and hollers of the audience became deafening as Violet and Anna battled, their elbows on the table.

Karen and Laura were now whispering with Daisy-Mae, who kept glancing at Jackie and nodding. Something was definitely going on.

She sighed, knowing they meant well. They didn't realize there was no man other than Cole who could capture her interest right now. She needed time to allow her crush—which had been reignited after being squelched only a few weeks ago—to wane.

Unfortunately, it seemed to be worse than ever. And even though she'd barely seen the man since April and Brant's reception, she thought about him much too frequently.

"Come on, girls, we need a winner!" Karen coaxed, as the wrestling continued, Violet and Anna turning red from exertion. Violet finally pinned Anna's hand to the table.

Karen beckoned Jackie and Daisy-Mae forward.

"Can we change the challenge?" Daisy-Mae asked. She fluttered her fingers, showing off her newly done nails.

"Are you stepping down?" Karen asked meaningfully.

Daisy-Mae nodded and returned to her seat. Jackie lifted her eyebrows in question. Daisy-Mae wasn't one to back down from a challenge. Not even over a fresh manicure.

Jackie was definitely being set up. But with who? She watched the bottom of the curtain, seeking hints. Maverick? The cute new hired hand on the Wylders' ranch? Or was Cole back there, her friends determined she make something of her very public crush?

Why should she win Cole, anyway? They weren't a good match. He'd been into rodeo, and she'd never owned a horse. She could ride, of course, but there really wasn't that much that she and Cole had in common.

And anyway, he was way too attractive. She could resist the man for only so long. If she won him, the whole thing would be nothing short of trouble. For both of them.

Jackie turned, waving Daisy-Mae back up front. Daisy-Mae shook her head, mouthing the words, *"Not worth it."*

"What if it's Maverick?" Jackie mouthed back.

Daisy-Mae frowned as though that was a ridiculous suggestion.

"Our second challenge is a handstand," Karen announced.

Jackie spread her arms again, looking at Daisy-Mae. As a former cheerleader, the woman could've had this.

"I can't do one," said Matty, returning to her chair.

"I'll hold your legs up for you," Jackie offered.

Because what if it *was* Cole behind the curtain? There was no way she was winning. No way.

"Bring it on," Violet Granger, the last remaining challenger, said with a giggle. Her cheeks were flushed as she bent over, placing her palms on the wooden floor. "Oh, man. My wrestling arm is spent."

Jackie watched with compassion. Violet had moved from Dallas to marry a man who'd left her at the altar a year and a half ago. By then she'd already bought a house and found a job with the town office, and had decided to stay. Now she was ready to move on, and had been flirting with Brant as well as Cole. This brave woman deserved a Wylder and all that their wonderful family brought with them. She deserved to win this one.

Violet was still folded over, butt in the air. That seemed to be the extent of her handstand.

"Need help?" Jackie asked, moving to her side. If the woman was willing to put herself out there, she deserved some help.

Before she could reply, Jackie hoisted Violet's legs in the air, holding her there for a second, until her arms started shaking and she squeaked, "Let me down! Let me down!"

Jackie helped her drop into a roll so she wouldn't hurt her neck as she collapsed. She lay there panting for a moment, then slowly climbed to her feet. "Your turn," she said, her arms held out to assist Jackie.

"No, no, it's okay. Knowing my luck, I'd kick you in the face." Plus Violet might be a bit too helpful and cause her to win.

"Here goes nothing," Jackie muttered, as the chanting reached deafening levels once more. Ensuring her sweater was tucked in, she pushed up her sleeves. She lifted her arms before swinging them down, planting her hands on the floor while kicking her legs in the air. Her handstand was awful, causing a crick in her back as she furiously waved her legs to keep them aloft.

Giggling, she tumbled onto the wooden floor, spreading her

arms dramatically. "That was awful. I think you should win," she declared, as Violet helped her up.

"I think you should. You did yours without help."

The audience was in stitches, and as Jackie performed a slow bow, she wondered why on earth she'd agreed to take part.

Oh, yes. Her car's broken bumper, which Clint Walker had estimated would cost her at least two hundred fifty dollars in labor, new bumper not included.

Violet stated, "You definitely should win."

"You're too nice."

"I know."

"I thought you'd be good at handstands."

"Maybe I had too much to drink," she confided. "The room is spinning a little."

Jackie was declared the winner, despite her protests, and Laura revealed the man she'd won. His black shirt emphasized the power of his square shoulders. His black hat was pulled down low, creating shadows across his eyes, and his jeans were so form-fitting several women in the audience nearly swooned.

It was none other than the man Jackie had been thinking about all her life: Cole Wylder.

* * *

Cole sucked in a deep breath and stepped forward, revealing himself to the crowd of waiting women. He immediately spotted Jackie and exhaled in relief as she studiously fought a grin that, despite her efforts, lit up her face. Irresistible.

She glanced away, looking conflicted, trying to hide the smile. He shook his head, quickening his steps. It was a good thing she didn't want him and he wasn't doing relationships, because otherwise he might find himself sorely tempted to sweep her up into his arms and kiss her. It would be way too easy to get lost in the way she brightened in his presence, and the way it made him feel as though he'd finally found someone who understood him, who had his back. Being around Jackie was heady and dangerous.

"Cole Wylder!" Karen announced, and the women cheered. Cole caught himself, almost stumbling. He'd forgotten about the other bidders. He paused long enough to perform a grand bow before continuing toward the woman he'd be spending Valentine's Day with.

"Jackie, I believe you already have Cole's number..." Karen winked at the crowd "...but the two of you can stand off to the side to make your arrangements for tomorrow's meet-up."

Cole could have sworn Jackie's chest expanded as she inhaled, as though needing to steady herself.

Good? Bad?

That smile was gone, her eyes filled with wariness.

Karen waited a beat as he cautiously closed the last of the distance between them. "Jackie? What do you have in mind for Cole tomorrow?"

He could've sworn the straitlaced librarian had a hint of mischief in her voice. She'd no doubt heard the rumors that Jackie had been crushing on him—even though she didn't act like it.

"I need my bumper fixed," Jackie said.

"Is that what we're calling it now?" Daisy-Mae exclaimed loudly. "'Cause I need mine fixed, too."

Cole chuckled as the room erupted with roars of laughter. A lot of women were trying to catch his attention, waving their numbers, and he was relieved he wasn't the last man being auctioned off today. He had a feeling a feeding frenzy was about to happen.

"So?" Jackie murmured as they stepped aside and the auction resumed. She ran her palms down the thighs of her jeans. She looked nervous and wouldn't quite meet his eyes. It was as though she'd read every thought running through his mind and feared he'd consume her.

"We meet again," he said mildly. Jackie was especially sexy tonight, even though she'd dressed down, as if not wanting attention. Or maybe she was well aware of just how eye-catching her sweater was, hugging her curves. Her cheeks were lightly flushed, giving her a healthy glow, and her lips looked delectable.

He knew he wasn't supposed to be wanting this, tempting fate and all that, but she'd gotten under his skin.

"I hear no hanky-panky is allowed," she stated, a glimmer of challenge in her eyes. She was no longer afraid to look at him, flirt with him. The change was surprising, sending him off-kilter.

"That shouldn't be a problem for us," he said in a low voice. "We've both sworn off of that."

"True. But what will we talk about if we aren't giving each other goodbye kisses?"

Oh, she was a flirt. She could hook him without even trying.

"That could be a challenge," he said gravely.

She smirked. "Maybe Karen has a book on conversation starters."

Cole laughed, his desire to take Jackie by the hand and lead her home growing by the moment. Although seeing a woman at a nearby table leaning off her chair, trying to listen in, sobered him quickly. He cleared his throat and said to Jackie, "Meet at eight? Your house?"

"Sure, but I don't have the tools we need to fix my bumper. Do you?"

"Why don't you come by the ranch instead? We've probably got everything we'll need. Are we replacing the bumper? I heard about your driving adventure from Henry."

"Is he still moaning about that? I swerved to avoid hitting Bill, and crunched my bumper when we hit the ditch. I have it taped in place so it doesn't drag, but I was hoping for something more permanent."

"Mom's having Clint over for supper again tonight," Cole said, referring to the local mechanic, his mother's new boyfriend.

It had been Clint Walker who'd phoned and asked him to come home, in an effort to win over Maria and show her how much he cared about her and her family. Cole thought that was pretty sweet. And he couldn't help noting the affection they shared with each other, something that had been missing between his parents in recent years. What they'd had in the beginning had faded thanks to time and the effort of running a ranch and raising five boys. "I'll ask his advice."

"He said I might need a new one."

"If we can't take care of everything tomorrow," Cole said, gliding his gaze over her face, "I take rain checks."

"I like rain checks," she whispered, her voice hoarse with what he recognized as longing. Her pulse throbbed under the thin skin of her throat, and she looked completely kissable.

For the second time that night Cole wondered why, when it came to Jackie, he was holding back and obeying his own rules.

4

On the morning of Valentine's Day, Cole hustled to complete the ranch chores, along with Levi, Myles, Brant, Ryan's hired stand-in, Blake, and the long-time hired hand, Hank, as well as Owen Lancaster, the newcomer. By the time the jobs were done, he still had an hour before Jackie was scheduled to arrive.

"Hey, you need help with that?" Cole asked Levi, hustling to lend a hand as his brother struggled to carry several long boards out of the riding stable to the ring. Apparently he wanted to get one more thing done before heading inside for breakfast. Or more likely he'd eaten before everyone, up well before dawn, as usual.

Owen came around the corner, saying, "I've got it." He took the back end of Levi's load before Cole could, instantly balancing the stack.

"Nah, I can step in," Cole replied. "You've got to help Clara over at Derkson's, don't you?"

Owen hesitated, no doubt doing the mental math on how long it would take him to eat, then get over to the other ranch to help his auction winner for the day. He stumbled as Levi continued on with the load.

"I've got it," Cole said, elbowing Owen out of the way and taking his end of the boards. "Jackie's meeting me here. Plenty of time for me to help and still get breakfast. You go."

"All right."

"And remember, no hanky-panky." He winked at Owen. At last night's auction, the twenty-something man had been bid on by an older widow. It had been sweet how kind he'd been about spending Valentine's Day with a woman nearing retirement. Owen had always been quiet, and he'd recently revealed a tender side that Cole figured the women of Sweetheart Creek would soon be swooning over.

"Funny," Owen muttered.

"I still can't believe Laura convinced you two to auction yourselves off like pieces of meat," Levi said with a laugh.

"It was for charity—the library," Cole said pointedly, as Owen jogged off toward his truck. The man lived on his family ranch, but for whatever reason no longer worked there.

"Drop 'em here," Levi said, as they reached a section of the ring's wooden fence where a few boards were rotting. Several aging planks had been replaced already, the new wood not yet protected against the elements with a coat of stain. "You and Jackie can take care of this."

"We're actually slated to do something else," Cole said carefully. When he'd first signed up for the auction, he'd floated the idea of himself and his winner helping around the ranch. Since Levi hadn't seemed delighted by the prospect, he'd found another way for them to be helpful. Basically, taking the charity event and spreading the goodwill even further.

"Cleaning saddles for the riding program?" Levi suggested, an edge to his voice as if he expected Cole to skip out for the day. "Helping Mom with the garden? Changing the oil in the tractor? Fixing fences?"

"I'll add those to my mental to-do list, but actually, we're working on something in town this afternoon."

"There's plenty to do around here."

"It's not like you'd let me."

"You own a fifth of this business."

"And you let me lend a hand with about point-five percent of it." Cole's voice was rising and he caught himself.

"Because who knows how long you're going to stick around."

"You'd think that would give you license to work me all the harder."

"I don't want to depend on you and have you up and leave in the middle of the night."

So him leaving without a goodbye was still bugging Levi. Noted.

"I left because y'all told me to." Cole placed his hands on his hips, daring his brother to argue that point. "You had some mighty bright ideas on the things I ought to do, and made a point of letting me know anything I thought might help my ex-girlfriend wasn't good enough. You didn't want to hear any other plans than your own." Levi had thought Cole should marry April, even though the baby wasn't his and April didn't want him any longer.

It had become clear to him that the only way to give April what she wanted—and needed—was to leave town.

Levi opened his mouth as if to shout at him, then clamped it shut, pinching the bridge of his nose. He was breathing like a bull preparing to charge.

Cole widened his stance, unsure what to expect. Levi was the bossy, know-it-all eldest, and not much of a fighter, but when he set his mind to something, that was it. No turning back. No changes.

"No, you're right," he finally said. "I had my own ideas on how you should resolve things and help April." He lowered his hand and met Cole's eye. "I'm sorry I didn't listen."

Cole exhaled, absorbing the apology in surprise. His anger faded, and his arms dropped to his sides.

Levi held out his hand, a spark of wariness in his eyes. Cole sighed and shook it, accepting the apology.

"Seriously, Levi. Make use of me around here."

"Overwork you, and drive you away?" Levi scoffed, dusting his hands together as he started toward the house, back straight and head held high with the assurance that he was right. "We just got you back. I'm not driving you away again."

"It wasn't you," Cole called after him. Fighting with Levi had been just one of the many pieces of straw that had sent this overburdened camel running.

"And if you ignore me, you'll drive me away again," Cole muttered quietly, following his brother. He had a feeling convincing Levi he could rely on him wasn't going to be as simple as a handshake and an apology.

* * *

Wearing a pair of red, heart-shaped earrings to celebrate Valentine's Day, Jackie turned down the gravel driveway to the Sweet Meadows Ranch. Nerves were battling excitement in the pit of her stomach and she muttered, "What am I getting myself into?" as she parked in front of the main house, her eyes scanning for Cole.

She was tempting herself. They had already agreed that the two of them were bad news, and suddenly she'd won spending today—Valentine's Day!—with him. Not that the occasion meant much to either of them, but still…

Him. Her. The most romantic day of the year. Working elbow to elbow for hours.

And last night, after she'd won him in the auction? She could have baked a pound cake in the heat pouring off them as they'd stood there, trying to act like two reasonable adults who weren't thinking about kissing each other.

Or maybe that had just been her.

Although Cole had had that smoldering look that seared her every time. The man was too hot for his own good.

She needed to have a word with Karen. Maybe even Daisy-Mae and Laura. Because as a proven matchmaker with a sizeable bag of tricks, she knew her friends had somehow rigged the auction.

Jackie parked her car and climbed out, promising herself she would not kiss Cole today.

Cole's grandfather was sitting on the front porch swing as though waiting for her. "Hi, Carmichael," she called cheerfully as she climbed the steps. A trio of dogs came around the corner of the patio, racing up to say hello. She bent to pet them all. Levi's Australian shepard, Lupe, Maria's new rescue, Bingo, and Myles's black-lab-and-Rottweiler mix, Buckey. Brant, now living with April, had his dog Dodge there, along with their new puppy.

"So? You and Cole," Carmichael stated, taking a sip of coffee.

"He's fixing my bumper today."

"Is that what the kids are calling it now?"

Jackie choked, and a twinkle appeared in the old man's blue eyes. "Have you been talking with Daisy-Mae?" she asked, thinking of how that same joke had played well at the auction last night.

"Most of those parts are plastic these days."

"I'm pretty sure all of Daisy-Mae is still what God gave her."

"I was talking about your car. You got a new bumper?" He eyed her vehicle as though judging whether she'd crammed the large replacement part inside the little sportster.

"No."

"Well, maybe the wrecker's open." He set the swing moving with a push from his scuffed cowboy boots. "There used to be a kid zipping around these parts. Same car. Same color, too. With any kind of luck he ran into issues with it, and it's sitting there waitin' for you with a good front end."

"That would be nice," Jackie admitted, moving toward the door. "Is Cole inside?"

"I reckon he's here somewhere." Carmichael was silent for a beat. "You know, if anyone can reach that boy, it would be a sweetheart like you."

Jackie backtracked from the door. "Sorry?"

The seventy-nine-year-old gave her a look, bushy white eyebrows raised. "Maybe there's a reason the two of you have been dragging your heels."

"Dragging our heels?"

"You'll be good for him. He needs some healing from a good woman." He peered at her with those startling clear blue Wylder eyes. "And you could use some healing, too, I reckon."

"Um, but we're not—"

"Don't look so surprised. Everyone thinks the world of you, JackieLynn. And Cole isn't half as bad as the rumors say."

"I know." She blinked back unexpected tears that had dampened her eyes at hearing her full name. There was something endearing in the old man's tone, and a sense of loss hit her hard. Her father used to call her JackieLynn when she needed encouraging. He'd bolster her with a few quick words, and had always possessed a sixth sense about when she needed them.

But these days she felt lucky if he recalled who she was when she visited. Every day she was thankful he hadn't turned aggressive with his Alzheimer's, as she was certain she'd be unable to bear it if he did. And even though it could be worse, it still wasn't easy.

"If I was the hugging type, I'd give you one," Carmichael muttered gruffly. His chin tipped upward, a display of stubbornness as he gazed out over the yard's expanse of dry grass.

"And if I was the type to take sympathy, I would accept it," she said, dishing it back.

Carmichael let out a grunt, the corners of his mouth twitching as though fighting a smile. She opened the front door, expecting it to stick despite Levi having repaired it several months ago.

"Get in there, and give that man a run for his money," Carmichael called after her.

That's what she was hoping to *not* do today.

She wiped her boots on the front mat and called out, "Knock, knock! Anybody home?"

"In here," Cole's mother called.

Jackie followed her voice to the kitchen, where Maria was at the counter, rolling out dough. The room smelled like pancakes and some delicious Italian dish like lasagna or spaghetti. The patio door near the large dining table opened and Cole entered, his cheeks rosy from the cool morning. He stomped his boots on the mat as though expecting mud to fall from them, then closed the door, his gaze on Jackie.

"Good morning. Need a coffee?" he asked, his voice rich and warm. He moved past her to the coffeepot after saying hello to his mom.

"We have a bumper to fix," Jackie said, checking the cow-shaped clock on the wall. "We're not going to sit here and sip coffee all morning until it's time to work on *your* to-do list."

"Taskmaster," Maria said with an approving laugh.

Cole shot them each a look.

"I like it," Maria said to Jackie. She jerked her chin in Cole's direction. "This one isn't like Ryan when it comes to skirting chores, but you may still want to keep an eye on him."

He threw his arms in the air as though indignant. "Hey! I've shown I'm someone to count on, have I not? I've been doing chores every morning since Christmas and helping Levi out as much as he'll allow."

"I thought he was eager for help from all the brothers?" Jackie said, accepting the cup of coffee Cole had poured for her. "At least Ryan sure complains about it a lot."

Cole, jaw set, filled his own cup. "He seems to believe I'm going to run off and leave him high and dry."

"You've still got that hint of a wild side," Maria said gently.

Cole set down his coffee and crossed his arms, then leaned against the counter facing his mom. "Have you seen it since I've come home?"

There was an edge in his voice, and Jackie watched the exchange over the rim of her cup.

"No, you're right," Maria said carefully, her fingers slowing as she formed a pie crust. She studied her son for a long moment, and Jackie sensed her concern. "You've changed. Five years is a long time."

"I'm sorry they slipped away," Cole said, his voice low with regret.

"Don't worry, Maria, I'll bring back Cole's fun side," Jackie said with a wink. "We've all missed it."

"I'm trying to turn over a new leaf," Cole growled. "I don't need an enabler. I'm not that guy any longer."

"Don't take yourself so seriously," Jackie teased. She was fairly certain that any new leaf Cole might turn over wouldn't have her on the other side. And that would be a good thing. "I'm not suggesting anything bad."

"I don't want you getting into trouble or starting rumors," Maria said, her moves brisk and efficient again as she finished with the crust and started adding sliced apples to her pie. "I just want to see you have some fun. You've barely smiled since you came home."

Cole gave an exaggerated grin that bordered on grotesque.

"A real smile." Maria's gaze bored into him. She looked as though she wanted to hug him and fix all his problems. "A mother wants to see her son happy."

"I'm working on it, Mom."

Cole and Maria locked gazes, silently communicating in a way that Jackie and her father used to. She focused on her cup, swirling the coffee around, waiting for their private moment to pass.

"Well," Maria said, a moment later, "I'm glad Jackie's here for the day. She'll help brighten you up."

Jackie's eyes met Cole's once again, a current passing between them, and causing her to look away.

* * *

"You doing all right?" Cole asked Jackie, after she parked her car in the equipment shed out near the barns. She was cute, wearing small heart earrings, jeans, boots and a teal top under a spring jacket. She looked beautiful, but also ready to work.

"I'm fine," she said, her tone light, an obvious lie.

"You seem quiet."

"Just thinking."

"About how you're supposed to cheer me up and fix me?"

"Ha." The furrow between her eyes deepened.

"My mom means well."

"I know."

Cole focused on studying Jackie's bumper, the idea that something was bugging her growing rather than waning. He didn't think it was just about his mother's hopes that Jackie be bubbly and fun, and somehow fix him.

"What are you thinking about?" he asked casually, as they squatted beside each other and started picking at the duct tape holding the bumper in place. He got his fingernail under an edge and pulled off a long strip, leaving a trail of gooey residue behind.

"You know. The usual," she chirped.

"And what's that?"

She gave him a wry look as though he should know the answer. "How to achieve world peace, of course."

He elbowed her and snorted in disbelief. She tumbled over, landing on the dirt floor. "Really? Was that necessary?"

"Entirely. You were lying to me." He dropped a knee to the ground to brace himself and took her hand, surprisingly warm and soft in the unheated building, pulling her upright as he stood. She straightened, dusting off the seat of her jeans.

"Need a hand with that?" he asked, tracking her movements.

"There's the Cole your mother missed. Can't think why she'd want *him* back." Jackie gave him a playful shove like she had when they were teens. He balanced himself with a quick shuffle. He liked it when she put her hands on him, and wondered if the push had been an invitation for him to reciprocate.

He returned his focus to her bumper, bending over rather than squatting. A few minutes later, he asked, "So what were you really thinking about?"

"I missed the memo that we're sharing our deepest thoughts and feelings with each other now," she retorted lightly.

"Why wouldn't we?" While his mom had been giving him a tough time there'd been a moment when Jackie seemed lost and sad. It was another small piece of the puzzle he was working on. Jackie was more than the well-known, larger-than-life-itself woman with the perennial smile, who'd never be knocked down by anything.

She faced him, hands on her hips, a satisfied smirk in place. "Great. Then tell me about this 'new leaf' business?"

Internally, Cole cringed. He supposed he had it coming, but that didn't mean he wanted to talk about it. There was too much left to sort out, too much shame over how everyone viewed him for his absence. He'd let many people down and built a reputation he didn't want to stand behind.

"I'd like people to see me differently than they currently do," he admitted when she stayed stubbornly quiet, waiting him out.

"Why?" Her surprise was clear.

"Why wouldn't I?"

"So you don't want people to think you're a fun-loving man?"

"Trouble." That's what they thought of his fun side. Someone whose fun had hurtful consequences, and that he didn't care.

"Or that you get things done, as promised?"

"And left my family holding the bag with the ranch? Or that I might be the father of Kurt?"

"Are you?"

"No."

"How about this image of you?" She twisted her lips playfully—pure Jackie—and he braced himself against the blow to his resolve not to kiss her again. "You don't want people thinking you're strong and handsome?"

"You think I'm handsome?" He waggled his eyebrows.

"You're missing the point."

"And you're missing the big picture. What kind of man has a whole town wondering if a four-year-old boy is his son?"

"Everyone knows Kurt isn't yours."

"He looks enough like a Wylder that people think he could be mine. And the way I left, folks think I ran out on April."

"Not everyone."

"And those people think I've come home to reclaim her." She'd eloped with Brant to prove to the world it wasn't going to happen. How crazy was that? Cole knew there were other reasons for the elopement, but he was certain that one had been pretty high on the list.

Jackie's eyes were dark, her expression serious as she asked, "And did you?"

"No," he said sharply. "You were there. You know Clint called me because my mom wanted me home."

"She does." Jackie's eyes softened. "We all do."

"My brothers sure have a weird way of showing it."

"They're afraid you're going to leave again."

"Well, if they keep shutting me out of the decisions about the ranch, I just might."

"So prove you plan to stay."

"How am I going to do that?"

"Buy a house? Marry a gal, or get serious with someone long enough that they'll think you're staying? Get them to relax, and voilà! It'll happen."

"Manipulate them?"

"Earn their trust."

He tore another strip of tape off the bumper, crushing it into a tight ball and tossing it at the tractor across the building. He stood and drew a deep breath. Winning back his brothers would be easier than rebuilding his relationship with his father.

Cole hadn't gone to his dad and Sophia's place the day after Christmas with his brothers, instead remaining home with their mom. His father hadn't reached out to him, and so far, Cole hadn't either. Roy had said some unforgivable things to him the night before he'd left. It had been a rough night. He'd then gotten in a fight with April, then with Levi. Then Brant.

There was a lot of trust to rebuild, a lot of forgiveness to spread around, and he was realizing time hadn't been his helpful friend in the ways he'd hoped.

"I think you're being too hard on yourself," Jackie said. "We all love you for who you've always been."

"Do you?" He turned to her, his anger with himself flaring. "Because maybe you should love someone better. What kind of son leaves his family and doesn't contact them for almost five years?"

He stalked over to the tractor, picked up the ball of tape and dropped it into a nearby trash barrel. He kept his back to Jackie, trying to move past his self-loathing.

"A man who believes he's doing the right thing," Jackie said, placing a hand on his arm. He hadn't heard her approach, with the dirt floor dampening the sound. "I know April asked you for some time and space to figure things out. Only a big man would've had the courage to step away from everything he'd ever known—his family, his legacy, his community and friends—to do that for someone he was no longer involved with. A man with a lot of love in his heart."

Cole felt the tension in his shoulders unravel before cranking up again. "She wasn't the only one who asked me to leave."

"Heath did?"

Cole shook his head. It hadn't been April's boyfriend, the father of her unborn son who'd asked him to leave.

"My family."

He closed his eyes, bracing himself. He hadn't admitted that to anyone. It was something he hadn't wanted to say out loud. It hurt too much. His father had said some truly awful things about his character, and that had hurt more than anything his brothers or April could ever say to him, or had. And it sure didn't help that his dad was acting as though Cole hadn't returned to town, to the ranch.

Jackie's jaw slackened. "I thought April..."

"I disappointed everyone," he said. "Let's leave it at that."

"Disappointed? Why?" Jackie asked. Her indignation took him off guard.

"For ruining April's life."

"And how did you do that?" She was rivaling his mother with her demanding tone. Clearly Jackie felt she could straighten him out. She might think differently if she had the full story.

"For breaking up with her," he said, watching for a reaction.

"You two were always breaking up."

"That time it was final."

"Because you were a poor match! It was just small-town proximity and convenience shoving you two back together again. Do you know how many people around here have gotten married because they couldn't find anyone better suited? Because they didn't have the patience to stay alone and wait for someone new to come to town?"

"Is that why you're single? You're patient?"

"We're talking about you, not me. But yes. I'm not settling for anything less than love. But you—" She poked him in the chest. "Breaking up with April was what she wanted."

"I know." He caught Jackie's finger so she wouldn't jab him again. "But my family felt I should've tried harder to make her happy. Held on to her. Given her a good life." He waited for Jackie's reaction to reveal what she believed.

"Yeah, and how did that obligation and effort work out for your parents? As I recall, they're divorced?"

Cole swallowed his surprise at Jackie's blunt, well-made point.

He lifted his hat and dragged a hand through his hair. "Well..."

Honestly, he'd been shocked when Brant had called him to say their parents had separated. And yet, somehow, he hadn't been surprised when his father moved on with Sophia a few months later. In retrospect, his folks had been more like partners than a couple. And sometimes you needed more than a partner.

And if you were April, you needed to throw yourself into something completely different in order to escape a man who had an unhealthy gravitational pull on you. Such as himself.

"April hooked up with Heath to make sure she didn't come back to me again," he said, hating that she'd felt the need to do so. Hating the judgment he would surely see in Jackie's steady gaze.

But when he looked, it wasn't there. Just fiery determination.

"It's called a rebound relationship."

"She got pregnant." He let out a shaky breath, remembering the night she'd told him. He'd felt as though he'd failed her somehow.

"So you're responsible for her proper use of birth control?"

Cole huffed impatiently. "You don't understand. She needed me to leave town so she could put her head on straight about what to do. What kind of man muddles up someone's brain and life like that?"

"She loved you. Like you love her."

"Loved."

Jackie blinked.

"Past tense. We're over each other."

Jackie licked her lips, then said, "What I'm saying is that she grew up with you. She didn't know anything other than Cole Wylder. Of course it was scary letting go. You were part of her family—her only family. Her life was your life, and what if your family took sides, and it wasn't hers?"

"She has parents."

"Yeah, but this ranch..." Jackie grew quiet, that sorrowful look in her gaze again.

"I appreciate you trying to make me feel better, but I do damage."

"So does she."

Cole blinked. "Don't speak ill of her just to make me feel better."

"Oh, shush," Jackie snapped, her eyes flashing. "It takes two and you know it. You and April are like bleach and ammonia. You're fine on your own, but when you're together too long, you make a toxic gas that kills people. How many lives did you destroy in your years away?"

When he didn't answer, she stated, "None." She did so with surprising authority, and all he could do was nod. He hadn't let anyone close to him, that's why.

But the way Jackie described what it had been like with April felt true. They were strong and capable on their own, but somehow when they were together everything went wrong.

Still, if he'd been a better man, he could have prevented sending her life off the rails like that.

"Together, y'all were just never quite right. Why do you think you were always breaking up? It was unreasonable of your family to expect you to be together forever. I certainly wasn't expected to stay with my first boyfriend. Or even my second. Or third."

Cole crossed his arms, leaning against the tractor, studying Jackie.

"Well?" she asked, her tone imperious.

"You're wrong."

She gave a long, exaggerated sigh. "So you're going to carry this around forever?"

He tried glowering at her.

"Fine, go ahead and give me that I-was-a-properly-raised-Texan-and-can-fix-and-prevent-everything excuse. You may have been raised right, but you're still human, and so is April. In fact, she was raised pretty much by the same people you were, so you can take your excuse and eat it."

Cole let out a snort of laughter, appreciating Jackie's feisty efforts on his behalf. The way she believed in him almost made him want to believe, too.

Without thinking, he closed the space between them, his cowboy boots bracketing hers as he pulled her in for a long-overdue kiss that sent searing heat all the way down to his toes.

* * *

Jackie rocked back on her heels as Cole broke the kiss. She looked at him for a long moment before throwing herself back into his arms, letting her lips do all the talking.

When they came up for air again, they stared at each other for another half beat before diving in for more. Jackie stumbled backward, propping herself against the tractor for support. Cole's body was pressed tight to hers and she snaked a leg around his hip, their kisses desperate. There was a need that thrummed and grew between them. A hole that could only be filled by the other.

Their lips were bruised, their breathing unsteady when they finally broke apart.

"We seem to be kissing again," Jackie gasped.

Cole watched her, his clear, bright eyes moving over her face as though he was wondering what to do next.

She had ideas.

She pulled his face toward hers, giving him a tender, sweet kiss.

The earlier desperation had waned, and the moment felt quiet, poignant. Something was changing between them, and Jackie wasn't sure what it was. It was scary and left her feeling vulnerable.

"You weren't just saying all of that to get me to kiss you, were you?" His tone was light, but a muscle in his jaw flexed, proving how serious his question was.

She placed her hands on his cheeks, trying to steady herself. "You've made sacrifices most men couldn't, or wouldn't. And I know you carry the burden of it."

He shook his head, as though not wanting her words to be true.

"There's no way you could have found the right path out of the situation with April, because there wasn't one."

"No. I could have found a gentle way to—"

Jackie covered his mouth with a finger, receiving an irritated look. "You have a lot of love," she whispered. "You have a strong desire to do right by the people you love." She tapped his chest above his heart. "I know you're not wild and flighty." She felt emotion welling inside her as she thought about all that Cole had sacrificed, the judgment he'd faced, both from himself and his family over trying to do the right thing.

They were quiet for a moment, and she smoothed a hand over the front of his jacket.

"You didn't leave because you didn't care." She pressed her hand into his chest. "You left because you *did* care."

Cole closed his eyes and lowered his forehead to rest against hers. When he opened them again, they seemed a paler shade of blue. "I want to believe you. You know how dangerous that is?"

"Then believe."

"Why do you know everything?"

"I don't."

"You seem to."

"I'm pretty good at sifting through the gossip, filling in gaps and figuring out the truth. There's not a lot of fun in a story about an honorable man leaving town. Those giggling geese prefer a tale about betrayal and shame. That's much more interesting than what really happened."

"And that is exactly why I'm trying to rebuild my reputation." He had straightened again, fire and determination returning to his eyes, strengthening the line of his jaw. "I hate that people think that of me."

"So how are you going to rebuild things?"

"I don't know yet."

"Yes, you do."

He relented. "I had plans. Show the town and my family I'm here to stay, that I'm calmer now and someone to rely on." He let out a soft, derisive huff. "But it only took me a week to get into a fight."

"The one with Heath on New Year's Eve? That wasn't a fight. You threw no punches. That was you standing up for your brother, and for April. Two people you care about, because you're an honorable, kind man. And it was pretty darn sexy, FYI." She dragged a finger down his shirt. It felt like every defense she made to try to convince him not to beat himself up was an argument on why she should love this man.

He grasped her finger, his breathing shaky. "Don't."

She met his burning gaze with one of her own. "Your grandfather thinks we can help each other," she whispered.

"How?"

"I'm not sure yet, but I'm pretty certain we'll know by the end of the day."

5

Cole couldn't seem to stop kissing Jackie. Only after she pressed her hands into his chest did he finally let up on the assault, stealing one last peck before reluctantly breaking free.

"Are you trying to duck out of working?" she asked breathlessly.

"Yes." He tugged her close again and laughed. "It's more fun kissing you."

"We're not supposed to be doing this."

"Hanky-panky stuff?" He caught her as she tried to weave out of his arms. There was a question in her gaze he couldn't figure out. "What?"

"You are trouble, you know that?"

He felt his smile fade.

"Oh, quit being so hard on yourself." She patted his chest, then ran her hands up into the hair at the nape of his neck, sending shivers down his spine when she gave a slight tug. Having her body snugged against his felt right.

"I was hoping you'd be at the auction," she whispered. She laughed when he studied her more closely.

"Maybe *you're* trouble," he mused.

"Maybe we're trouble together," she retorted, kissing him lightly. Sadly, she broke the kiss before it could get out of control. But her fingers were still stroking the fine hairs on his neck, running up his skull, giving the short tufts a light tug as she explored. The sensations she was creating were doing funny things to his brain, and he was finding more reasons to keep Jackie around. After all, his family liked her, and maybe having a steady, kind girlfriend would help him earn back trust. It would be like Jackie had suggested earlier—show everyone he planned to stick around. Being committed to Laura seemed to have made Levi even more committed to the ranch and its prosperity. Cole's family could likely extrapolate the same intentions from him if he exhibited similar settling-down behavior to his older brother. And he'd know it was working if Brant gave him a dog. His veterinarian brother tended to do that when he accepted and trusted someone. And so far, no dog for Cole.

"What was that my grandfather told you about us helping each other?" Cole asked, a fuzzy idea forming in his mind.

She shrugged, her tone offhand. "He thinks we can fix each other."

"You're broken?"

Without answering, she slipped from his loose embrace and went to crouch beside her car, wiggling the bumper. "Do I need a new one?"

Cole stared at the task in front of him, his motivation waning. Suddenly the idea of dating Jackie to solve all of their problems seemed juvenile. What was the point of trying to be a good guy when nobody was likely to see it? For many he would always be the wild Wylder, even if he no longer acted like it.

"Want me to call the wreckers?" he said finally.

Jackie nodded, and soon they were standing among acres of old vehicles stacked in the Texas scrubland several miles east of Sweetheart Creek. They worked side by side, retrieving the same shade of blue bumper from a sports car before returning to Sweet Meadows Ranch.

Now, sitting on the equipment shed's dirt floor, Cole scratched his chin. Buckey, Myles's dog, came ambling in, tail wagging. She threw herself down beside Cole, placing her head in his lap. He absently scratched her chin before pivoting onto his back to slide under the car to attach the new bumper, the dog crawling under with him.

"Do you remember which bolt goes where?" he called to Jackie.

"No."

"How about you?" he asked Buckey. The dog shuffled closer as if to take a peek.

Cole angled himself to look out at Jackie. Making a funny face, she gave the bumper a thump, fitting it back into place so he could bolt it in.

"Careful!" he yelled when she gave it another thump. "Don't set off the airbag!" His warning caused Jackie to jump, and he laughed while Buckey scrambled out from under the vehicle.

Jackie's eyes widened before she exhaled and rolled her shoulders at the prank. Earlier, for safety, they'd disconnected the battery and airbags. "You're a brat."

"You don't like working with me?"

"You said it, not me."

Cole let out a huff as though annoyed. Hanging out with Jackie was easy, and he hadn't expected how smoothly they could flow between moments of heat and moments of camaraderie and partnership. It reminded him of Levi and Laura. They flowed like they'd been together longer than the few months they had.

Cole knew he should feel awkward for having revealed his fears and past mistakes to Jackie, but instead he felt closer to her. Was that how Levi felt with Laura? He and his older brother used to talk about all sorts of stuff, and Cole had missed him during his years away. Had Levi missed that, too? Had Laura stepped into Cole's role like Jackie was stepping into Levi's? Was this a part of growing up?

Still, there were some things you could say to a brother you just couldn't say to a woman. And maybe one day, if he stuck around long enough, he and Levi would find that common ground and trust again.

Cole attached the last bolt and rolled out from under the car. Standing, he dusted himself off, then stretched, clasping his hands behind his neck while curving forward to relax the muscles in his lower back.

He tapped Jackie gently on the shoulder to draw her back from where her thoughts had taken her. She had crouched to hold the bumper, and was still hunched over, hands on the blue plastic even though it was now securely bolted. He offered her his hand, helping her up.

"What's next?" she asked, squeezing his biceps in that friendly way that always made him want to flex his arm.

"It's fixed. We just have to reconnect the battery and airbags."

"Thank you!"

Her gigantic grin had him leaning in to place a kiss on her lips before he thought better of it. It was a quick one, but Jackie's features softened with pleasure.

Cole exhaled slowly, realizing what he was doing. He'd spent his years away being careful not to get too close to anyone, not to get attached, not to let someone get hurt. He needed to fix things with his family and within himself before he got involved. And here he was, making Jackie promises with each kiss. It didn't matter that they'd said they weren't doing this; their actions were writing checks reality would never cash.

And yet every time he kissed Jackie he felt as though he was getting closer to some vital truth, adding another piece to the healing puzzle.

"About what you said earlier about me needing a girlfriend..."

he began, wondering if his plan to remain alone, ready to jump when his family asked him to, was a poor one.

She laughed and bumped her shoulder against his arm. "Cole, you're not looking for a girlfriend. And I don't do short-term relationships anymore. So don't get all serious on me just because we keep having little moments."

Her happy expression clouded, and she turned away, collecting the tools spread over the floor.

Cole felt strangely rejected, and he took a moment to watch her work.

But what if he *wanted* a girlfriend? Jackie would meet all of his requirements, plus some. She was smart and funny, easy to work with as well as hang out with. And he'd be lying if he said he wasn't attracted to her.

He couldn't help but think once again that there might be validity to her idea of dating someone—like Jackie—to show the community he was stable and serious now, intent on staying in town and building a life for himself.

"I can hear you thinking all the way over here," Jackie said.

"Yeah? What am I thinking about?"

She'd straightened, a collection of wrenches bunched in her hands. She studied him with her pretty blue eyes. "You think you're a mess."

"I am a mess."

"But you need to remember that dating me—a flirt—would only reinforce the worst rumors about you." She dropped the wrenches in the toolbox with a clatter, bringing Buckey running over to check on her.

"You're too hard on yourself," he murmured. Jackie was well-loved, and with her past history of not dating anyone seriously it would only add weight and meaning when she finally did. And that small fact might help her, as well, as he'd learned over the years that there was nothing like a woman being taken off the dating market to make men feel as though they'd lost out on something. If he were to date Jackie—even as a ruse—it might just show the town that she was more than a flirt, and bring her Mr. Right out of the woodwork. "A relationship would show I plan to stay."

She didn't argue, nor agree.

"Something slow and steady. Something to demonstrate I've grown up." He sighed, leaning against the tractor again. "I'm tired of sitting around, waiting for a chance to prove myself to Levi. That's not working, but a relationship might."

The problem was that a steady relationship came with expectations. A ring. A house. If he didn't settle down with the woman, it would appear as though he hadn't changed. And anyone he approached would think he was looking for either a wild and crazy time or something serious, when all he wanted was to calm everyone's minds about why he'd returned home and who he'd grown up to be.

He needed a woman who didn't want forever with him, and wouldn't demand the things he couldn't give. He needed someone like Jackie, the town sweetheart, where if she chose him it would mean something—and not just because she'd been publicly chasing him for years. He needed a woman who wouldn't cause him to ruin the reputation he was rebuilding. Someone who could play the game, help him move toward his goal, without tripping him or herself in the process.

"So find a girlfriend," Jackie said lightly, not looking his way. "I'm fairly sure you have a lot of options."

"I don't want a lot of options," he mused. He rubbed his mouth, a hint of strawberry lip balm from Jackie causing him to focus in on her again.

He needed someone who wouldn't get serious. Someone like Jackie. Because despite what everyone thought, she could take him or leave him.

There was only one woman for the job. Only one woman he would enjoy being with for several months while this played out.

He needed Jackie.

The idea was as powerful as a bull kicking him in the thigh on a dismount.

* * *

"Will you be my girlfriend?" Cole asked, with such earnestness Jackie's heart nearly stopped working.

"What?"

"I mean, as a fake. You know, like you were saying earlier."

"I did not suggest you lie to the town and your family by faking a relationship with someone, and especially not the local flirt. That doesn't show you've changed. And trying to trick them—"

"No, I don't want to lie," he said quickly.

She froze, swallowed hard. "So you'll tell everyone your relationship is fake?" Or did he mean that his feelings were real? Feelings about her? The woman he'd asked to stand in as a girlfriend.

"No... I..." He wiped a hand over his mouth as he'd done moments ago. "Okay, so it would be a lie. But I was thinking a relationship that was real, or real enough, but with an agreement that it won't go anywhere."

"Still fake. Still a lie." She shook her head. The man seriously hadn't changed. Would this latest bit of knowledge finally allow her crush to die? Now that she could see with clarity that he wasn't good for her?

"It's just dating. Without the wedding or blowup at the end. I need to show I'm putting down roots."

"Buy a house."

"You know you'd be perfect." He eased closer, with a soft look meant to convince her, no doubt.

"Because I'm a flirt? Because I don't have feelings?" This was like April telling her to throw herself at Cole. Nobody seemed to think she wanted love and commitment. He was choosing her because she wouldn't complicate things, and there'd be no sticky, troublesome feelings like love.

"Because I like you. Because I trust you."

The earnestness in his gaze shook her resolve.

She focused on the toes of her cowboy boots, centered her thoughts on the reasons he felt she would be perfect for something fake, then focused on the resulting pain.

"Because I don't do long-term, serious relationships?" She ignored the fact that she always ended it before anyone ever got close to love.

"Jackie, this could help both of us."

She saw it so clearly from his point of view that all she could do was shake her head. "Because this is fake, there won't be a big blowout. Things will naturally fade away. Right? You'll look like you gave me a shot, like a nice guy, and I'll look like I finally caught my Wylder."

But she'd be one step further from finding her own happily ever after.

"Will you think about it?"

She sighed, knowing she couldn't avoid considering the angles. A fake relationship would do both of their images good, and maybe it would finally show men she was worth considering, if Mr. Uncatchable chose her for more than a fling. And maybe people like April would stop laughing off her desire to have love and a family. Sticking with one man for a while would likely be good practice, too. It might also help her hone in on what she was looking for in a life partner.

"I suppose," she said thoughtfully, "anyone who thinks you're still angling for a way to get April to return to you—"

"I'm not."

"—will give up that line of thinking, because you and I will be some hot new thing."

"And exclusive?" he asked, a possessive set to his jaw that surprised her.

She moved to the hood of her car, using it as a seat. "Who said I'm agreeing to this asinine idea?" She crossed her arms and glowered at him, letting him know she was still the boss.

The problem was that now all she could think of was what would cause him to want exclusivity.

Well, it would be bad for their images if they were dating others on the side, obviously. This ploy would be about his reputation, not about him wanting her all to himself for some primitive reason based on obsession or emotions.

"Of course exclusive," she said with exasperation. "We're aiming to build a good reputation."

She eyed him, that handsome angle of his jaw, the way the brim of his cowboy hat shaded his eyes, giving him a look of mystery. Her anger faded, and a feeling of futility washed over her.

"It would also help beat off all those women drooling after you. I mean, after all, it's just a matter of time before you weaken and give in."

She studied her boots again. She wanted this. She wanted Cole all to herself. And ever since their first kiss, her desire to have a shot at a relationship with him had been renewed with an unrelenting vigor. An honest shot. Just one. And knowing this was all he could give, she would take it.

The bright side was that a relationship with him—even fake—would be an expedient way to crush the obsession she'd had for him all her life. In her experience, there was nothing like dating someone to dim her fantasy and send her running in the opposite direction.

She studied Cole carefully. So handsome. So rugged. Could it be that easy? Date the man, spend some time in his arms, and poof! The crush faded and she could move on?

Was it possible that eligible men sensed she was holding a

candle for someone else, and that was what kept her from finding love? The crush was all a daydream, but that didn't matter. She'd made her heart unavailable. And it was time to free it with a dose of reality.

Cole was looking at his own feet, his hat hiding his expression.

She cleared her throat. "The point is…" She softened her tone when he glanced up warily, waiting to hear what she had to say. Waiting for her to reject him, cut him down. Her heart softened even further. "I want you to succeed at winning back your family and the town." She realized how true that was. He'd made so many sacrifices, and instead of being celebrated, he was being punished. "And a relationship might help, as well as serve as a protective shield against…" She paused, unable to say something he might find negative or derogative.

"Womanizing? Bad decisions? Brawls? Drunken rages?"

She laughed. "That's not really you. Never was. And drunken rages? Really?"

"There's still time."

She smiled at his joke and he shrugged good-naturedly.

"You really think I can keep you in line? Make you look respectable?"

"If anyone can, it's the town sweetheart."

She laughed again.

"You think I'm lying?"

"You might be a tad overly optimistic."

"I thought that made me charming." He quirked his head to the side. "No?"

Jackie moved to him, wondering if they could really pull this off. She toyed with the collar of his shirt, her gaze scanning him, noting details. Kissing him would be no issue, and ditto for spending time with him.

It might also put a halt to those pitying looks. It was no secret people thought she was a lovesick fool who'd spent the past several years pinning her dreams on a man who would never even notice her. Was it wrong to feel a thrill at the idea of walking around town with a certain level of look-at-me-now, I-wasn't-so-wrong?

"How long would we keep up the charade?" he asked, his voice a deep rumble, his hands coming up to cup her elbows. His touch registered inside her like a Richter scale needle during an earthquake.

"I haven't agreed to temptation and deception."

"Temptation?" he breathed, his lips inching closer.

"Always." She cleared her throat and straightened her spine. They both knew she was going to say yes, but she wasn't going to let him distract her with a mind-clearing kiss while they were still bargaining. They needed to set some pretty serious parameters if they were considering deceiving the people who mattered most to them. "What qualifies as a long-term relationship these days?"

"How many months was your last one?"

She shook her head and grimaced. "Yours?"

"Nope." He shifted. "So?"

"Two months?" That didn't feel very long.

"Double it?"

She nodded with a shrug.

"So you're mine until June?"

His words sent thrills and fear through her in equal measure. "Wow, that's quite a while."

"Can you handle that much of me?"

"We may find there are some weeks where we need to spend more time at work."

"You really can't do four months with one man?"

"Of course I can." That was what she was looking for, right? Practice. "That's just a lot of Cole Wylder."

"I thought you were rooting for me."

She smirked.

"You'll pay for that." He pointed a finger at her, trying to act threatening. Her smirk grew.

"We seem to do okay as friends. And to preserve your sanity let's say the end of May as our goal—three and a half months. I'm sure we can survive that."

"Friends who kiss a lot," he said, giving her a smug look. "But what about you?" He tipped his chin in her direction. "Would this cramp your style?"

She rolled her eyes. "There's no style to cramp."

"So to reiterate, we want to look serious, but not too serious."

"Too serious?"

"Like we're on the marriage track."

"Right."

"I just want my brothers to understand I'm here to stay."

"Nobody will expect you to marry me. Or vice versa."

"Right. I'm too wild and crazy to settle down?"

"Nobody's come close to marrying me." She frowned, considering how others might view their relationship. "Maybe this won't work."

"I think us finally getting into a relationship that's steady has a certain power to it," he said. "It'll show everyone that we are *both* ready for this. That we've both outgrown our old images." He slid his hands around her waist, as though hoping to settle her. "You're the only one I can do this with."

"I know."

"So will you?"

"Almost four months?" She exhaled slowly, her heart thumping.

"Please?"

She gave a tiny nod, accepting the inevitable.

He released her with a grin, then held out his little finger. "Pinkie swear. A couple of months together. No blowups. Just kisses and image reform."

She gave him a look of disbelief. "Really? A pinkie swear? If anybody in town saw this right now, they'd throw out your old reputation in a heartbeat."

He frowned at his finger, and she snagged it quickly, releasing it before he could react.

"Yep. You're a tough bad boy. Pinkie swear," she scoffed, heading out of the equipment shed, her heart thrumming in her ears with what she'd just done. What she'd just agreed to. "I'm hungry. Is it lunchtime yet?"

He hurried after her. "Girlfriend, wait up."

When she turned, she didn't know whether to look at him or away.

"Feels weird, doesn't it?" he said.

"Because you made it weird." Her entire chest felt warm with the idea that of all the women in the county, Cole had chosen her as his girlfriend.

* * *

Cole saddled up two horses, one for himself and one for his girlfriend.

What a strange feeling it was having a girlfriend again. Someone he trusted. Sure, it was a fake commitment, but he was certain he'd enjoy the process.

Like a real couple, they were heading down to the creek for a Valentine's Day picnic before their afternoon odd-job task.

As Cole adjusted the saddle blanket on his horse, he glanced to the right, where Jackie was untangling a bridle she'd dropped on the dirt floor moments ago. His girlfriend.

Technically, he could kiss her anywhere, anytime. Well, maybe. They hadn't quite ironed out the rules yet.

He smiled to himself. Despite the way his thoughts had been drawn to Jackie ever since he'd arrived home Christmas Day, he hadn't seen a relationship coming.

And even though it was fake, and neither of them wanted

something lasting, he hoped the idea helped them both. That Jackie's Mr. Right finally saw what he was missing, and that Levi realized Cole intended to stay, as well as show the town he was ready to settle down and act like a mature adult.

He tightened the saddle, then stroked his horse's nose. Lots of people in Sweetheart Creek seemed to think Jackie had an undying crush on him. Was there a chance she was in this for real?

Somehow, despite the heat between them, he didn't think so. She flirted and had fun, but she'd made it clear she didn't want something permanent. And by no means had she jumped into his arms when he'd suggested she pose as his girlfriend.

They mounted their horses, and he turned down a dusty trail that took them through pastures where cattle grazed, and along to where Sweetheart Creek ran through the property. He'd spent hours riding this and the other trails on the ranch during the past several weeks, becoming reacquainted with his home while unspooling his thoughts.

Despite it being winter in Texas, the afternoon sun was warm. And while he missed the extreme seasons of Colorado, where he'd spent most of the last year and a half, he took comfort in the predictability of milder weather that wasn't out to murder him should he be caught unprepared.

The creek came into sight, the sound of water babbling over rocks joining the soft thump of horse hooves.

"How about here?" Cole asked, indicating a grassy area near the creek. In the far distance clouds were gathering for the week of rain his mother had mentioned was coming. The temperature would likely drop to near freezing tonight, making this the last perfect picnic day in a while.

"This is pretty romantic, you know," Jackie replied, swinging one long leg over her saddle and lowering herself to the ground.

He did the same, then took her reins and hitched the horses to an oak growing along the creek's edge. The frequent spring floods overwatered it, pulling at its roots before abating, leaving the tree still standing like a lone survivor along this stretch of creek.

"I have to up my game. We're official now." He shot Jackie a wink that sent a flash of color racing across her cheeks. She had grabbed a straw cowboy hat from her car and looked every bit the Texan she was. She could go from a boot-scootin' boogie in the saloon to her desk job at the feed store, to riding the trails or getting dusty under her car's broken bumper. There was something about Texas women that he just hadn't found in anyone else during his travels.

"Don't go getting me all hopeful," she teased. "I might start expecting flowers, chocolates and…" She shrugged as though embarrassed.

"Hanky-panky?" he asked, shaking out the picnic blanket on a flat patch of grass.

"Karen said we're not allowed."

"Maybe she could make an exception."

Jackie flashed him a glare and pursed her lips, but her gaze dropped to his belt buckle.

As Cole set out the picnic, he said, "This is about where Ryan got swept downstream when we were kids. He was seven, I think." Cole had been about thirteen, in that strange age between dependence and rebellion. He'd still wanted to be close to his parents, under their wing and tightly woven into the fabric of the family. But he'd also craved independence and had possessed a healthy desire to buck their approval.

"I heard the story," Jackie said.

Cole settled on the blanket, elbows on his knees. He tipped his hat back and scratched his forehead as familiar feelings of not doing the right thing, of letting his brothers and himself down, came over him.

"It was a flash flood, more violent than any I'd ever seen. The creek covered the ground we're on now, plus another couple feet." He gestured to the dry land behind them. They had been working at keeping a nearby herd safe from the floodwaters and had taken a break. Levi had stalked off earlier, having gotten fed up with his four younger brothers teasing him for kissing some girl Cole couldn't even remember. Ryan had kept throwing sticks into the creek for Bonkers, the family dog, and Cole had snapped at him, stressed out at being the responsible brother in what was a dangerous game of fetch.

"Ryan had been trying to cross the creek and suddenly he just slid in and disappeared. Couldn't even see a flash of his shirt."

"Myles jumped in after him though, right?" Jackie asked, kneeling beside Cole on the blanket.

He nodded. "Then the dog went in, too. He got dashed on some rocks." Cole scanned the area, looking for the outcropping they'd thought had killed Bonkers in the flood. "Bonkers showed up the next day. Broken leg." Cole felt that old twist in his gut, the immeasurable guilt for not searching for the family dog. He'd been washed down the creek to who-knew-where, then had limped the long miles home. They'd all written him off instead of looking for him.

Cole cleared his throat. "Dad wanted to put Bonkers down, and Brant lost it. I don't think the five of us ever agreed on anything so fast in all our lives as we did that day. We pooled our allowance and Christmas money so we could take Bonkers to the vet."

He swallowed over a sudden lump in his throat. He was talking about stuff that was so far in the past it no longer mattered, but he didn't seem able to stop.

"Brant ran to the house to get Mom when Ryan fell in the water, and I just stood there, frozen, not knowing what to do."

"Where was Levi?"

"He'd gotten tired of us teasing him, and left us to finish the chores. He'd been dating some girl. Well, not dating her, but he'd kissed her, and we'd found out." Cole sent Jackie a crooked grin, thinking about the good ribbing they'd given Levi. There was nothing quite like teasing a sibling. You could be unrelenting and yet know you'd be forgiven, still loved at the end of the day, still someone they'd go to the end of the earth for.

Unless they were forced to choose between family members—even ones not related by blood. Then all bets were off.

He didn't begrudge his family's opinions, or how they'd argued with him over what he should do about April all those years ago. They'd been fighting for the family member who'd needed protecting the most—April. And Cole would have done the same had his position with his family been reversed.

"And Levi's never had time for women ever since," Jackie mused. "At least until Laura showed up."

A lot had changed for the brothers on the day of the flood. Brant had found his future career, Ryan had decided his brothers weren't worth listening to, and Cole had figured out some important things about who he was.

Back then, he'd always been Levi's shadow, second in command, feeling important by proxy and as though he could do anything his older brother could do.

Yet that day he'd failed at keeping his brothers on task, keeping them safe. Cole had frozen in shock, while both Myles and Brant took immediate action. Without Levi there barking at him, Cole had been locked with indecision, unsure how to fix the situation.

Shortly after, he'd joined the rodeo in an effort to find his own path and to force himself to make split-second life-or-death decisions while on top of livid bulls.

"I've never really heard the ending to the story," Jackie said, drawing him from his thoughts. She had settled in a cross-legged position, her left knee resting against his. "Just that Myles and Ryan were swept down the creek, Brant got bounced around in the truck when your mom floored it across the pastures, and that Ryan thought he should have crossed elsewhere."

"Eventually he and Myles came up against a downed tree." Cole pointed downstream. "I managed to grab them."

"I thought you said you froze?"

"I did." He'd stood there staring in panic when Myles had jumped in. Then, not knowing what else to do, he'd run down the creekbank following alongside.

"But what could you have done? Jumped in as well?" She handed him half a sandwich from the lunch bag they'd packed in a saddlebag.

He took a bite.

"Maybe your role was to do exactly what you did—run downstream and catch them when they passed under a fallen tree? Then haul them out?" She gave him a wry look. "You're too hard on yourself."

"They would've found somewhere else to climb out," he said, tossing a piece of breadcrust toward a squirrel that had come down the angled oak, curious about the newcomers.

"I dunno. I've heard the story, as I said," Jackie stated with a healthy dose of skepticism. "Myles told me he was half-drowned by that time and wasn't sure they were going to surface again if they went under. He said he couldn't reach the branch and was saying his last prayers when you appeared out of nowhere and pulled them out, like they were no heavier than teddy bears."

Cole could still feel the wrench in his shoulder as he'd grabbed Myles's outstretched hand, locking his fingers around the stone-cold ones of his brother. The momentum of the current had jerked him half off the fallen tree. He'd hooked his legs around branches he couldn't see, his abs straining as he'd stretched, fighting the force that wanted to drag him off the thick trunk. One split second of error could have sent him into the current along with Myles and Ryan.

Like in rodeo, adrenaline had kicked in, giving him strength to do the impossible. He'd yanked Myles, then Ryan out of the water, hauling both brothers from the danger sucking at their boots like a hungry beast. Their lips had already been a frightening shade of blue when he'd pulled them onto the fallen tree. The rapids below had been rushing, frothing brown water ready to consume them all, and he'd all but thrown Ryan onto dry land.

His youngest brother had coughed up an impressive amount of water. Could Ryan have survived in that swollen, freezing creek for even a minute longer? How much strength had been left in Myles's muscles to keep them afloat?

"It sounds like you boys worked as a team," Jackie mused. She wrapped her fingers around Cole's forearm and brought him back to the present.

He nodded, suddenly no longer sure why he'd felt like such a failure in that crisis. Maybe because he hadn't barked out commands like Levi would have done. Maybe because he hadn't been the one to jump in without a thought. He'd been a stronger swimmer than Myles, who was four years younger. But he'd also been strong enough to pull his brothers from the frothing waters, which Myles might not have been able to do.

Maybe it had worked out the way it was supposed to, and what he felt now was simply the fear that had dug in deep with its claws while he'd stood on shore at a loss. It was a terror that had tainted everything about the memory for him up until the present moment.

Cole placed his hand over Jackie's, willing himself to make peace with the memory. A better man would have prevented the whole thing from happening, just like a better man would have been able to prevent the mess he'd made of April's life.

But he wasn't that man. He was himself.

And maybe somewhere in the retelling of this tragic tale he'd figured out that there might be more to April's story, too.

* * *

Jackie sidled closer to Cole on the picnic blanket. She tried to picture the quiet creek trickling past as swollen and dangerous.

She wasn't going to "fix" Cole, as Carmichael predicted, but she could listen and be a friend.

From her perspective, Cole had done exactly the right thing and kept a cool head with the whole Ryan-in-the-creek incident.

"Why are you still beating yourself up for Ryan falling in?" She gestured to the slow-moving water.

"Because it's not the only time I've frozen during a crisis."

"You mean it's not the only time you've waited for your moment to make a difference?"

Cole was silent, and Jackie feared she'd broken the train of thought that had been allowing him to open up to her.

"When April broke up with me, I let her run off. She was more angry with me than I'd ever seen her. If I'd acted, she and Heath wouldn't have... She went down some really hard paths because of me not acting in that moment."

"So you felt you should have cooled her down and somehow prevented what happened with Heath?"

Cole readjusted his hat with a jerk, looking up at the cloudless sky, then back at the creek. He seemed antsy, his knees jiggling.

"She adores Kurt," Jackie said. "She would never wish him away. She's right where she's supposed to be, with Kurt and Brant, and that might not have happened if you'd tried to stop her."

"I'm not wishing Kurt away." Cole's eyes flashed.

"I know. But without all that stuff with Heath, I'm not sure she would have seen Brant for the man he is. The man she needs."

Cole let out a huff, sounding almost amused. "He broke the bro-code."

"The what?" Jackie giggled before catching on to what Cole was saying. "Oh. Do you mind that they... got involved?"

She could see Cole mulling things over. He was frowning thoughtfully, shaking his head back and forth as though he couldn't find one reason to be bothered that his brother had found true love with his ex-girlfriend.

Ever since age six, when Jackie had first noticed Cole at recess, she'd watched how he would pause and think. Kind of like Brant, but different. Brant was soft and gooey on the inside, whereas Cole had this hardness about him. A certain go-get-it-done-and-take-no-prisoners approach—after he'd contemplated things and charted his course.

She admired that about him. He was like a train on the tracks —not about to take a corner that wasn't already plotted out ahead of him. And yet he'd veered a few times in his life, showing her he wasn't so rigid that he couldn't change his mind, and reset his trajectory when needed.

Tired of waiting for a verbal answer, she said, "You know, maybe you're blaming yourself for stuff that nobody else does. Things work out the way they're supposed to."

"And it's like that in your own life?"

She paused, thinking of the things she'd like to change. Her father's health, her own loneliness.

"Of course," she said mildly.

"Are you always this much of a know-it-all?" He frowned at her, his eyes shaded by the brim of his gray Stetson. It made his angular jaw seem even more hardened and firm. He sure didn't look like a man intent on changing his mind at the moment.

"How long have you known me?" She batted her eyes, and his narrowed.

"Basically, all my life."

"There's your answer then." She released his arm, realizing she'd been clutching it, and dusted her hands together, turning to the packed lunch. "Shall we stop fussing over the past and enjoy more of my favorite lunch?"

Maria, the sweetheart, had made chicken salad sandwiches and cinnamon buns, leaving the meal in the fridge for them.

"So much for the prodigal son getting pampered upon his

return. How'd you charm my mom?" He shot Jackie a quick grin that made her feel warm and liquid inside, as if he'd kissed her.

"That is for me to know and you to find out."

He growled low and fake lunged for her. She squealed and giggled, tumbling onto her back, knocking the bag. Cole sprawled over her, bracing his weight on one elbow, then dropping a kiss on her forehead.

"You missed," she informed him.

"Are you always this demanding?"

"If you think this is demanding," she said, running her hands up his deliciously toned sides, "you just wait and see."

He chuckled and rewarded her with a kiss on the lips, one that was sweet and slow. The kind that curled her toes and left her wanting more.

Jackie sighed. She could spend all afternoon wrapped up in this man.

"Too bad you have chores for us after lunch," she grumbled.

"I'm going to make you muck stables."

"Really?"

"No."

"Then what?" She hoped this was his afternoon plan for her.

"It's in town. A good deed."

Now she was really intrigued. "Does that mean we need to rush?"

"Not at all." He lowered his lips to hers once again and slid his fingers under the hem of her shirt, gently stroking the skin above her waistband.

"Just don't make us late for supper," she said breathlessly. "I bought tickets."

Cole's fingers stopped moving and he frowned. "Supper?"

"The Valentine's Day meal. It just seemed like… I don't know. Karen asked." She bit her bottom lip, panicking, knowing it seemed presumptuous to buy the add-on dinner tickets for what now looked like a romantic date. She'd been in full help-out mode when Karen had asked if she wanted two, and she'd said yes without consulting Cole first.

Cole shifted and sat up.

"Where are you going?" she asked, alarmed that she may have already broken a rule, and that Cole would call things off before she had a chance to get over her feelings for him.

"What are our boundaries?"

"I don't have any." She gripped his shirt and pulled him back down on the blanket.

His look of surprise had her laughing.

He kissed her slowly, then said, "You totally have boundaries, sweetheart."

"Sweetheart?"

"You don't like it?"

She did. But it was dangerous ground, judging how it made her feel. She didn't remember him calling any of his old girlfriends "sweetheart." Was that something he did for his fake girlfriends, or did it mean she was special?

"It's fine. Just unexpected."

"This entire day has been."

"Amen to that." And then she kissed her fake boyfriend as if he was real.

6

Cole adjusted his watch and paced outside Jackie's bedroom door, inexplicably nervous about their dinner with the other auction winners at the community barn.

She'd promised she needed just one more minute.

That was five minutes ago.

When he'd arrived ten minutes ago, she'd still been wearing her dusty jeans and dirt-smudged long-sleeved shirt from their day of chores. She'd even had a small twig still stuck in her sandy-yellow hair, from working on Mrs. Fisher's yard.

While he'd gaped at her, she'd handed him her dog's leash. He'd taken Goose for a meander through the nearby park behind the gas station. Now they were back and she still wasn't ready.

Even though Cole had told Karen and Laura he needed his auction winner to help with ranch chores, he'd actually been planning a surprise for Mrs. Fisher. With her husband in a wheelchair, and her working long shifts at the diner, her yard had suffered over the past several years. Myles and Brant had been helping out as they could, but there had still been a lot to do, from weeding the flowerbeds to trimming back the lawn overgrowing the walkway, as well as reshaping the hedge.

Jackie had been game, even charming William Fisher, who'd come to the door, into agreeing that they could work in his yard as a surprise for his wife.

But what had Jackie been doing in the forty-five minutes since they'd parted ways at the Fisher's? Was she experiencing cold feet? She'd been flirting with him all afternoon, claiming there were no boundaries between them.

Maybe she'd realized there was nothing to be gained by faking it as his girlfriend.

Then again, she was a fun gal, a flirt, and didn't seem to mind kissing him. And Sweetheart Creek could be a tad boring.

However, he'd flown home after their work, grabbed a fast shower, shaved, and upended his clean-laundry pile looking for his nicest pair of Levi's and cleanest shirt. He'd dug through the box of belongings he'd left behind on the ranch to find his most-prized belt buckle, which hadn't ended up in his bag when he'd left town. He'd even begged his mom to show him the iron, so he could run some heat over the shirt. Then he'd taken a hat brush to his best Stetson, removing dusty fingerprints from its brim, and swiftly oiled his newest boots.

He looked good. Real good.

And Jackie hadn't even seemed to notice.

He paced her living room again, stopping at the kitchen counter to help himself to a glass of water. There was a note by the sink, and his eyes caught a few words before he minded his own business.

Memory care facility.

Knowing he shouldn't, he drew the scrap of paper closer, reading the careful, flowing handwriting. He sucked in a breath when he saw the dollar amount at the bottom of the note.

Had Jackie come home and dealt with figuring out care for her ailing father instead of getting ready for their fake date? She hadn't mentioned Gerry Lee once during their day together, but Brant had said in passing that her father wasn't well.

Cole downed the last of the water, mulling over how he might help Jackie.

She came hustling out of her bedroom, breathlessly saying, "Ready."

She froze when she saw his expression. "What?"

He couldn't seem to make his jaw do anything but hang there. She was gorgeous. Seriously gorgeous. Levi's former-fashion-model girlfriend had nothing on Jackie. Nothing. Unable to stop gaping at her, he didn't even try. Those wonderful legs, the flare of her hips, the nip and tuck of her dress at her waist, the hint of cleavage at the softly revealing neckline. Irresistible.

"What?" she demanded.

He blinked, rousing himself. "Did you paint your nails?"

She held them out for inspection, then gave them a shake and blew on them. "They're still a bit damp. Do you mind driving? I don't want to ruin them."

"Sure." He took her in again. Her shoulder-length hair was done up off her neck, her makeup subtle, highlighting her cheekbones and her sparkly, mischievous eyes.

She was hot. Seriously hot.

"How did you do all of this in..." He checked his watch. "... eleven minutes?"

"If I knew you were timing me, I would've done it in ten." She glided past him to the door, leaving a fruit-scented trail.

"What do you smell like? Raspberries? No... strawberries?"

"It's my lip balm."

"I can't wait to taste that."

"We're late. And it's cherry."

Cherry. She was trying to kill him.

As they trundled down the stairs to the gravel parking area behind her building he asked casually, "How's your dad?"

"He's in Riverbend."

Not what he'd asked.

"How long's he been there?"

She spun around. "Where's your truck?"

He gestured to the end of the alley, where he'd parked on a cross street. It was already dark out and he shifted closer, ready to steady Jackie should she stumble on the uneven ground in her heels. "Is he doing all right?"

"Do you know where we're going?"

"I heard he has Alzheimer's?"

"You can park behind the building," she informed him as they reached the sidewalk. "There's a guest spot."

For visitors. For boyfriends. That idea felt inexplicably good. As if he belonged somewhere. Was expected, even welcome.

Cole gave up trying to get answers about Jackie's dad and opened the passenger door to his F-150 for her. He'd bought the truck secondhand when he'd returned home, and while it had seen a lot of miles before him, he doubted it had ever met a woman as stubborn as Jackie when it came to things she didn't want to talk about. Her father must be in bad shape for her to so doggedly avoid the topic. She was like that mare in the ranch's riding stable that always sidestepped a saddle. What was her name again? Roses?

Jackie focused on something out the side window while he climbed in behind the wheel, and Cole got the feeling she was hiding.

He paused for a second, considering the bouquet of flowers tucked on the dashboard. He'd bought them on a whim on the way to Jackie's, but somehow this didn't feel like the right time to give them to her.

Everything at the moment felt too real.

And they weren't doing real.

Instead, he embraced the silence and reached out, squeezing her hand. Her fingernails were slightly tacky, but she didn't withdraw, or complain about the fact that he might be messing up her manicure.

"Do your toes match your fingernails?" he asked.

"No, that's why I'm wearing boots."

He chuckled. She wasn't wearing boots, but the jut of her chin told him not to point that out. He pulled onto the street, lifting the fingers of his free hand off the steering wheel to give Sheriff Johnson a casual wave as they passed. Then checked his mirror to see if the officer was going to follow him, call him out on the gradual angling away from the curb he'd made due to his right hand being tangled in Jackie's. The police truck remained where it was.

"If you ever want to talk about your dad, I'm here."

Jackie gave a curt nod, her fingers tightening around his.

"I know how it feels to be alone, and it isn't much fun."

"You don't want to hear about that stuff," she said, lifting her right hand to toy with a slender chain around her neck.

"Maybe that's what boyfriends do. They dump the crap from their past on you, so you can dump your current crap on them."

His chest felt tight, this moment seeming surprisingly important to him. He wanted her to trust him, to open up and be her true self the way he had been with her all day. Because he had a feeling that as open and generous as this woman was with everyone around her, there was a secret wall holding the real Jackie inside.

"Let's just enjoy the evening," she said tightly, "and not pretend to be more than we are."

"We're not friends?"

Her eyes fell on the bouquet.

"Those are for you." He waited as she tentatively reached for them, drawing them into her arms to inhale their fragrance. "Sorry, they were out of roses."

"I like these better. They're free of expectations, and can just be their own beautiful souls."

"Kind of like you?"

She laughed at his attempt to be sweet, filling the cab with the best sound he'd heard all day.

* * *

Reaching the community barn, Jackie hesitated on the threshold. Cole, coming up behind her, clasped her hand in his. Her mind was still stuck in the phone call she'd had with her father's physician, Dr. Gomez. He no longer felt the level of care available at Gerry Lee's nursing home was adequate. And while Jackie had known the day would come, since the center didn't have a special unit for residents with dementia, she hadn't been ready for it to come so soon, or for the gut punch situation that had resulted in the call.

Earlier in the day, her father, lost in a world she no longer recognized as this one, had found his way out of the nursing home and had nearly been hit by a car. Luckily, Riverbend was a relatively small town, and the driver turned out to be an old friend of her dad's, and had brought Gerry Lee back to the facility. She didn't know what she'd have done if her father had gotten lost in a city where no one knew him, and been left to meander about on his own.

He couldn't stay where he was, and Dr. Gomez recommended he be moved to a memory-care facility designed for Alzheimer's patients, with dedicated, trained staff. But how was she going to afford that? Her dad had some money left from the sale of his house, but there wasn't enough if he proved to be as physically resilient in his golden years as he had during his prime.

Cole gave her hand a tight squeeze as she continued to waver in the doorway. "We don't have to do this," he said.

She straightened her shoulders, pushing away her doubts and worries, hoping that in a few minutes her false cheer would feel more real. Stepping forward, she reached in her pocket for the dinner tickets and handed them to Carly, who was seated at the entrance to the beautifully decorated barn.

"They roped you in, too?" Cole asked her.

"Ryan and I are very romantic, aren't we?" she said, with a wry smile that warmed as she cut her eyes to the youngest Wylder. He was leaning against a pillar, arms crossed and looking bored.

"I suggested going somewhere for Valentine's Day," he protested, coming alive.

"You *are* somewhere," Jackie teased. She glanced at Cole and did a double take. The man was seriously hot tonight. She'd barely focused on him earlier—other than to note that he looked even more handsome and irresistible than usual. But now that she had a moment to do nothing but soak him in, she felt her knees weakening.

His shoulders looked extra broad in the black dinner jacket he wore over a crisply ironed gray shirt that brought out the intense blue of his eyes. His jeans were more worn than his dark wash ones, but somehow looked dressier paired with the jacket. The outfit made him look casually confident and extremely handsome.

Her crush was not waning one bit right now.

Cole was watching her with a curious gaze, no doubt trying to hone in on what had been bothering her. He'd almost managed to get her to cave and spill her problems. His kind, patient questioning had been close to irresistible. It had taken every scrap of resistance Jackie could muster to keep her mouth shut, because if the old problem-solving Cole had surfaced and come up with a plan to save her and her father, she would have fallen irreversibly in love with him.

And that was a terrible plan.

Anyway, she was with him to fix *his* life, not the other way around.

"Shall we present ourselves to the town?" he asked as they left the ticket table, leaning close enough that she could smell his aftershave.

She laughed nervously, the charade suddenly feeling very real. People were going to freak out with excitement and tell him she'd been pining for him for years. Which would be fine if they truly were in love. But because they weren't, it was only going to make things awkward. And when the two of them eventually "broke up," everyone would pity her for reaching for the unattainable and failing.

"You all right?" Cole asked, when she didn't answer his earlier question. He seemed worried about her, and the very idea gave her the strength to shake off the rest of her mood. She was here with the handsomest man in town. He had made an effort to dress up, to be an actual boyfriend, asking about her, bringing her flowers. And now he was holding her hand.

She straightened her shoulders again. "Of course."

As soon as Karen Hartley spotted their interlinked hands, she beamed. It didn't take more than a few seconds for others to notice, as well. As Jackie followed Cole between the long tables set up under the strings of lights, past the cutout paper hearts and Mason jars filled with tiny lights littering the white tablecloths and along the creaky wooden floorboards, she could feel people watching, her back prickling.

"This is certainly romantic," she said. It felt a lot more like a community date night than dinner for a bunch of people who'd spent the day working hard on chores to support the library.

She didn't dare look at Cole as he murmured in agreement. The barn was nearly full, with at least fifty people already seated. The two of them were late, and it felt as though nearly everyone was noticing them. As they passed full tables on their way to a partially empty one at the back, she could hear snippets of whispers. Her name. Cole's. April's. Words about Cole's sudden return.

Cole said, "Maybe I should just give you a big, long kiss and end the speculation?"

Jackie laughed. She didn't realize he was serious until his powerful hands grasped her waist and pulled her against him. His shirt was smooth under her palms, his muscled chest warm and firm.

Cole angled his lips onto hers, his hat surely blocking everyone's view even though there would be no doubt as to what they were doing. His arms slid farther around her, holding her so close a piece of paper couldn't be slipped between them. Jackie freed her hands and slid them over his shoulders, marveling at his strength before gliding her fingers into the fine hair at the nape of his neck, her favorite place. His tongue teased her lips, and she opened, deepening the kiss. She wanted to wrap her legs around him and let him carry her away. As his mouth angled over hers, kissing her deeper, she wondered if he was thinking the same thing.

When they broke apart, she stumbled against a chair behind her, then used it for support.

Wow. That was worth the wait. So far every kiss had been.

Kissing Cole was definitely not her crush's kill switch.

Cole caught her again, pulling her against his chest. This time it was a brief, sweet meeting of their lips, but still powerful.

"Well," she said, her voice shaky, when they broke apart.

"How is it that every time we kiss it's hotter than the last?" he murmured in her ear, his body humming against hers, his breath sending shivers down her spine. She could feel the heat of attraction coming off him in waves, and she longed to take him away from here and keep him all to herself tonight. They hadn't set out any rules yet, but she was certain that would be on the No list.

"How fast do you think we can eat supper and get out of here?" she asked.

She saw his attention flicker to movement off to one side. Servers from the local caterer were setting filled plates in front of those who were already seated.

"I'm thinking twenty minutes or less." He stroked her jawline with a thumb, her body still snugged against his.

"Our goal is fifteen." She winked at him. "Speed-eating contest."

"You're romantic, despite what everyone else says," Cole

declared with a laugh. He quickly pulled her to a free seat and held it out for her, no doubt brushing off just how serious her offer had been.

Which was a good thing.

This was fake, a long game. It was not a fling, and she'd be best to remember that so she didn't ruin everything.

* * *

Cole would have to be blind not to see the way Jackie was a magnet that attracted male gazes as they'd crossed the dining area. Sure, plenty of women were gawking, eyes flicking over them, but that had been to gather fuel for gossip. The men, though—they'd followed only Jackie as she'd marched across the room, moving like she owned the place even though she was being towed by Cole.

He'd given her that kiss to make it clear to all that Jackie Moorhouse was off-limits. And wow, it had been quite a kiss. His body's reaction to that hot and sultry lip lock had nearly had him skipping supper and tearing out of there, Jackie tossed over his shoulder.

But he'd been raised better than that. Just barely.

Plus Jackie was taking the plan to mend his reputation seriously, and it wouldn't have done hers any good to rip out of here after a kiss like that. Everyone would think he was using her, and that the crush they all said she'd had since elementary school was causing her to be blind. He had to do right by her. He had to be the kind of man a woman like her deserved.

As they waited impatiently for their meals to arrive, Cole settled in next to Jackie, dropping his hat on the table and draping an arm over the back of her chair. Across from them, Daisy-Mae sat with a partially bald man, both looking uncomfortable. Beside Daisy-Mae was Jenny Oliver, whose attention seemed to drift to a different table with an interest that meant, well, interest.

"So?" Daisy-Mae asked, elbow set beside her plate as she leaned forward. "You two?"

Cole waited, expecting Jackie to confirm their status as a couple, and ignoring the way Daisy-Mae was watching him. He could practically hear her questioning the excuse he'd given her not that long ago about not wanting a girlfriend. And here he was with one.

When Jackie remained silent, he said, "I finally let her catch me." He gave her a warm smile, surprised when her cheeks flushed. "I avoided her for years at recess, but now I'm wondering why."

"So you're staying in town then?" Daisy-Mae asked, doubt thick in her tone.

"I am."

"He found a reason to stay," Jenny said with a sigh, as Cole took his thumb and grazed it along Jackie's bottom lip as though tenderly wiping something away. Jackie swallowed hard, then took a sip from the water glass beside her plate.

"You're a couple," Jenny said softly, her focus still split between them and another table. She peeled her eyes away from whoever had her mesmerized and flicked her gaze between Cole and Jackie, her confusion and concern growing. "For real?"

"For real," Jackie echoed.

Jenny continued to stare at them, along with Daisy-Mae, and Cole snugged Jackie closer, planting a kiss on her temple. She gave a quick smile and glanced over her shoulder, then back at everyone's plates. The other four had their meals already and were politely waiting for Cole and Jackie to be served before starting.

"Go ahead, your food is getting cold," she told them.

"Well, I say way to go, you two. It's about time," Daisy-Mae said sincerely, lifting her fork.

"I need to find someone next," Jenny complained, following suit.

"Nope, Jackie said I'm next," Daisy-Mae protested.

The men sitting beside them dug into their food, not seeming bothered that Cupid hadn't delivered for them today, as their two dates bickered about finding true love.

"What did y'all do for odd jobs?" Cole asked Jenny as their plates arrived.

"Dennis helped me with inventory in my store."

The man nodded, remaining silent. His cheeks had colored and Cole wondered if the bratty twinkle in Jenny's eyes meant she'd had him working in the lingerie section just to make him uncomfortable. She was quiet and kind, but had a bit of a bratty streak to her when someone rubbed her the wrong way. It had made her one of Cole's favorite people back in high school.

"How about you, Daisy-Mae? What did you get up to?"

"She helped me tag a herd this morning," the man beside her said, leaning back and slinging an arm behind her. When his fingers curled around her arm Daisy-Mae straightened as though correcting her posture, moving out of reach.

Cole lowered his chin, raising his eyebrows in question, until she gave a slight shake of her head. He knew she was well-practiced at handling men and unwanted attention, but that didn't mean there weren't times when it would be nice to have a man step in on her behalf, ready to raise a fist.

By the time Cole had finished catching up on everyone's day, his plate was half-empty. He checked Jackie's plate. It was scraped bare.

"I told you, fifteen minutes," she said.

He pressed his leg against hers as he checked the time.

"You seem to be eating rather slowly," she drawled, causing his blood to warm. Was she serious?

No, she was a flirt.

This was all a game.

He laughed, relaxing in his chair. He was going to enjoy the next several months. That is, if he didn't die from internal combustion whenever she gave him that teasing, burning gaze. One that had him thinking of things that would most definitely not fall into the category of fake relationship.

* * *

Jackie could barely focus on the chocolate cake that had been served after the main course. Her friends kept shooting her looks of encouragement laced with concern. She could read their thoughts like they were her own. Daisy-Mae was excited for the way she was finally claiming the object of her affections, but wondered if she'd get hurt by hooking up with a known heart-breaker. Jenny was thrilled Jackie and Cole appeared to have a connection, but wondered if it was fueled by something other than love on Cole's part.

Jackie hated to admit it, but spending time with Cole today had not nudged her any closer to ending her crush. The man was as good as she'd dreamed. Everything from taking care of Mrs. Fisher's yard without being asked, to worrying about her father, to loving his family so much he felt guilty for not being able to pull his brothers from the raging creek faster, to being a thoughtful and caring boyfriend tonight. He was everything she'd look for in a man.

Which meant she might have messed up.

She gave herself a shake. No, this was all still early on, and it was a charade. That's what she needed to focus on. Heck, Cole was probably pretending. He couldn't possibly be like this day in and day out.

It was like her Jackie Show. He was putting on the Cole Show to prove to his family that he was home for good, loved them and wanted to fix things.

He'd signed up for the Jackie Show, not for her to fall in love with him. And especially not with a pretend version.

She opened her mouth, smile at the ready… and couldn't think of a single thing to say.

Cole scooped up a chocolate-covered strawberry before his dessert plate was swept away by a busboy. He held it out for Jackie. "Want my strawberry? I noticed you saved yours for last."

She took it, watching him. His gaze was full of kindness and warmth that stirred her crush like a cat pouncing into a cloud of butterflies.

"Are you okay?" Jenny leaned forward in concern as Jackie slowly ate Cole's strawberry, lost in her thoughts.

"You've been really quiet," Daisy-Mae added.

Jackie faked a yawn and stretched her arms. "I'm beat. That's all."

"Sure, sure," Daisy-Mae said with a wicked grin, shooting Cole a sly look.

"Sorry, girls." She shifted in her seat, grabbing her purse from where she'd slung it over the back of her chair. "I'd love to stay and chat, but I need to teach Cole a few things. It was on his to-do list." She stood, winking at her friends, who hooted with laughter. The men beside them gaped, eyeing Cole, then her.

Cole's face turned red.

"I'm kidding! Cole and I…" She lowered her chin, looked at him shyly through her lashes. "…are just taking things slowly. We discovered today that we get along really well and enjoy each other's company." She frowned, realizing the truth of that statement. "So we're exploring where that might take us." Also relatively true.

"Well, judging from that kiss earlier, I think I already know," Daisy-Mae said with a giggle.

"They're serving coffee," Cole said, giving Jackie a pointed look.

She dropped her purse into her lap, realizing what she'd done to him. She'd put on her flirty-and-full-of-games, innuendo-making persona, which was not the image they'd planned to create. No burning fast and hot. Slow. Careful. Like they wanted this to last. And she'd retreated into safe territory as soon as things got a little too close for comfort.

Jackie sighed.

This was so difficult. Who was she supposed to be? Her real self? Nobody was ready for that.

And if she let down her guard, she might fall in love with this man.

"So? Did you get Jackie some flowers?" Daisy-Mae asked, resting a hand under her chin. "It's Valentine's Day."

"I did, actually."

Jackie felt herself blush, and looked down. He'd not just bought her flowers, but had inadvertently chosen her favorites. When she glanced up again her friends were watching her.

"You two are so sweet," Daisy-Mae said.

"Us?" Jackie asked in surprise.

"You're so… different tonight, Jackie." Daisy-Mae was studying her. She focused on Cole with a look of wonder.

"I'm not. Just worn-out, that's all."

"She's had quite a day." Cole slipped his hand around hers and gave it a supportive squeeze while meeting her gaze. The kindness in his expression brought tears to her eyes.

No. No, she wasn't going to cry. She wasn't going to mistake his caring for something deeper.

She laughed, getting out of her seat. "I'm tired. We'd better head out."

"Already?" Jenny complained.

Cole shifted in his chair, seeming reluctant to leave.

"I need a good-night kiss from my boyfriend, and since I'm tired and it's going to be a very long kiss, we need to start now." She winked at him.

He stood, jaw flexing, and with a sweep of his hand indicated she should go first. She patted his cheek on the way by and added an exaggerated sway to her hips.

At a narrow spot between two tables, his hand landed on her lower back to guide her, and she felt as though she almost lost the ability to walk. When they reached the doors, Cole collected their coats, then held Jackie's out for her to slide her arms into. He turned her to face him, straightening her collar, then pulled it gently but firmly toward him, drawing her in for a long, deep kiss that did nothing to help the strength of her legs.

"What was that for?" she breathed when the kiss ended.

"Just reminding you of something."

"What? That you're my…" she paused, then lowered her voice "…fake boyfriend for the time being? I think everyone already noticed."

His jaw flexed. "No, that when you're with me you don't have to act like you're alone and scared."

She felt her eyes dampen unexpectedly, and she whirled and headed outside before anyone noticed.

She was *not* scared.

"Good night," Cole called to Laura and Karen, who were bent over a list near the doors. He joined her outside. The rain Maria had predicted was going to start soon, judging by the feel of the cold, damp air.

"I'm not scared," Jackie said, her voice hard.

"Then what is it?" Cole had put his hands in his pockets, watching her from under the brim of his Stetson.

"I don't want to end up looking like a fool."

"I don't want that, either."

So he thought it was possible? Somehow that made it worse. She pulled in a deep breath for courage. "I like you, Cole. Everyone in town knows that."

She waited for his reaction. He shifted his weight, but continued to listen.

"They're waiting for me to get my heart broken. And that kiss…" Her voice got shaky.

"Which one?"

"Both. All of them! I can't act like I don't get Jell-O knees when I kiss you." She laughed, suddenly embarrassed. "You're a really good kisser. I'm affected, and I don't want everyone to think I'm falling in love with you. Most of all you." She pressed a hand against his chest and leaned in slightly. "We have to keep this light."

He nodded. "But I thought we were acting like this was a real, committed relationship and not some fling."

"I'm not acting like this is a fling!"

"The jokes, Jackie. Quit acting like you're scared of something deep, and this is just some itch we're scratching."

Right. She'd done that.

"I just don't want everyone thinking we're a super serious thing heading toward true love, because otherwise when we break up they're all going to be like 'Oh, Jackie! Are you okay? You just failed at the love of your life!' You know?"

The evening had grown cold, and Jackie pulled her coat tight around her body, like a shield. Her voice was shaky again when she said, "And in there it felt like we were dancing too close to pretending this is the real thing, when it's not. You're very caring and sweet."

"And you don't like that?" Cole gently unfolded her arms, then zipped up her coat. She felt frustrated and cared for at the same time. His head was still lowered, his hat blocking his face, as he said, "So you want to show everyone that we're in a relationship, but it's fun and light and you're never going to fall in love because I'm actually a big meany who doesn't know how to treat his girlfriend?"

His serious, flat tone made her pause. She felt the hurt in her heart when she said, "Yes."

He nodded slowly and stepped back, hooking his hands in his jeans pockets. His wounded expression speared her.

"I mean, no. I just… This is harder than I thought it would be."

"So you have to act cool and unaffected?"

"I don't—" He made her sound like a crazy person.

"Even though my kisses make you want to rip my clothes off and worship me for the rest of your life?" His lips quirked, his eyes dancing in the light coming from the barn.

"You…!" She gave him a playful shove. He was doing what she did! Making light of the moment, turning something serious into a joke.

But she knew he understood. They were inching along a precarious high-wire, with no safety net below.

He pulled her under his arm with a chuckle. "Don't worry, sweetheart, I have that effect on women. I'd be worried if you were immune to my seductive nature."

She snorted and tried to slip free, but he tightened his hold.

"I promise I'll go easy on you," he murmured.

She had a feeling he understood the power of their kisses and the impact. It was deeper than anything physical.

"You're going to ruin me," she said, thinking how all future men would pale compared to this one, who was steadying her world with a simple embrace.

"Maybe you should get out while it's easy."

"That would be cruel."

"It would?"

"If I left you now, you'd be crawling back to me by next week. It's best we carry on until you're good and tired of me." She slipped her arms over his shoulders, warming her fingers under his collar, against his skin. He didn't shiver, just took the cold like it didn't impact him.

He spun her up against the side of the barn and pressed his body against hers. "Not unless you crawl back to me first."

"And why would I do that?" she said with a breathless laugh.

Suddenly, his lips were on hers, one hand gliding down her hip to pull her snug. She kissed him back, working her fingers under his jacket and yanking the hem of his shirt from his pants. She placed her cool hands on the heat of his lower back, marveling at the muscles, and the slim channel of his spine. He groaned into her mouth, shifting his hips to meet hers better.

"Hmm. That is a good reason," she said, her earlier worries melting away. She wanted nothing more than to enjoy this moment, in the arms of the man she'd dreamed about for many, many years.

7

Cole hooked his boot on the bottom rung of the corral's gate and watched the horses graze, thinking about Jackie. Although worrying about her was more like it. There was a lot going on with that woman, behind her sunshine smile. He'd expected them to spend time together this week, but she'd been silent, so he'd taken his cue from her. However, if they didn't go out soon, their relationship would begin to look odd. And over. But he knew he couldn't act first, not after he'd seen the fear darting in and out of her eyes at the Valentine's Day supper.

He wasn't sure what to do about that other than let her put up her boundaries, and then respect them to the best of his abilities. This wasn't a real relationship and he didn't have the authority to barge in and fix her, or change things like he wanted to.

But that was fine. Her boundaries would remind him to keep his distance and focus on winning back Levi's trust. Cole dusted his damp leather gloves together, then loaded up the tools for fence mending, intent on keeping himself busy proving to his family he was interested in ranching and was here to stay.

Even if Levi was still a bit reserved about giving him more than a few odd jobs on the ranch, he knew his mother liked having him home again, and they'd had some good conversations. Her new boyfriend, Clint Walker, was a nice guy, too. He'd called Cole up a few days before Christmas with a request on Maria's behalf, asking him to come home. Clint had called him "son" and had offered to buy him a ticket, letting him know he planned to pick up Cole from the airport on Christmas Day.

Somehow, despite Brant calling him every few months to fill him in on things that were happening on the ranch, or to ask if he was ready to return home, having Clint ask had made the difference. Logically, it made no sense.

Maybe it had simply been time to return. Or maybe it had been knowing he had an impartial party in his corner, one who wasn't likely to weigh in on the drama, that had finally given Cole the courage to test his reception back on the Sweet Meadows Ranch.

Truly, he'd never regretted leaving, as it had been a classic case of damned-if-you-do-and-damned-if-you-don't. Everyone had felt certain their own opinion on how to help April was the correct one, and despite the mess, Cole was glad he'd listened to her and given her space.

She was moving on, and that gave him hope that he could, too. When he looked at his mistakes from someone else's perspective now, he could see that maybe he'd done what he had been supposed to do. Even though he still felt he should have taken immediate, heroic action—both with April and her unexpected pregnancy, and with Ryan in the flooding creek.

"There you are." April and Kurt were walking his way in their boots, jeans, thick jackets and cowboy hats, ready to ride, by the looks of it.

"Speak of the devil," he said.

"What?"

"I was just thinking about you."

"You were?" Her eyes narrowed cautiously.

"And me?" Kurt asked, his face beaming with hope.

"Yup. You, too." He swooped him up into the air and the little boy's laughter lifted Cole's heart. Yeah, one of these days he wouldn't mind having a few kids of his own. He'd teach them how to ride and be a cowboy or cowgirl.

"Your mom said you were out here, and that you'd be able to find your grandmother's saddle blanket for me. Levi had it repaired and Maria wants me to bring it back to the house when we're done our ride."

"I bet it's in the tack room or Betty's office in the stable."

April shook her head. "Maria said it's packed away in the loft."

In other words, somewhere April could easily find it, but Maria was trying to make him feel useful. It had truly come to this, hadn't it? His mother meddling behind the scenes to set things up in a way that would make him feel included.

"She also wanted Carmichael's saddle cleaned and stored up there."

"He's giving up riding?"

April shrugged. "Until the dry season, for sure."

That made sense. His grandfather would be eighty in a few months and Cole had noticed the way damp weather locked his joints up tighter than a cowboy's fist in a fight over a pretty woman.

They began walking toward the stable, and Cole noted that April was looking a lot happier than she had a few weeks ago. Marriage seemed to suit her. A lot better than it had on the day of her wedding reception, when he'd caught up to her during a trail ride. She'd been feeling lost, and he'd been able to guide her, he felt. It had been nice to help out.

"How are things?" he asked, when Kurt ran ahead to catch Tootsie, the orange mama cat that had the run of the ranch.

"Good."

"Yeah?" He slowed his pace, and she stopped moving.

"Really good, actually." She didn't look up at first, but when she did, he could see she was hesitant to talk to him about her marriage.

"Brant's a good man."

"I know," she blurted.

"I'm glad you found each other, and I know my return hasn't been easy for either of you."

"It's fine."

She was such a poor liar.

"April?"

"Okay, okay. The rumors weren't awesome." She'd crossed her arms, and was chewing on the corner of her mouth. "But we took care of them." There was a telling ghost of a smile playing at her lips.

So they *had* eloped to defeat some of the gossip. He chuckled, knowing that without the rumors it might have taken the two of them years to get to the point of marriage. Some things were just meant to unfold, messy and ill-timed, but ultimately for the best, weren't they?

"I'm sorry for what happened with Heath," he told her.

She watched him, eyebrows raised, waiting for him to explain.

"I'm sorry I wasn't a better boyfriend and that you…" He'd thought about this long and hard, made several speeches in his head, but somehow none of them felt right.

"Cole?" She touched his forearm. "It's fine. Really."

"No, I caused you pain. I hurt you, and for that I'm so sorry." He watched regret flicker in her eyes.

"I'm sorry, too."

"Why?"

"Are you serious?" She was giving him attitude with a strength that took him aback.

"Yes," he said cautiously. "I am."

"Cole." She shifted impatiently. "You weren't the only one in that relationship. I hurt you, too."

He opened his mouth to argue.

"I did." She said it with conviction. "I should have been stronger."

"You shouldn't have to be strong when you're with the man you love." He cleared his throat. That sounded too present tense. "That you cared for."

"Yes, I should. Strength is needed to balance relationships." Her gaze was fixed on the stable behind them. He got the sense she was thinking of the present as well as the past. She turned her focus back to him, her look serious, mature. Strong. "We never balanced."

That was one way of putting it.

"I sometimes think that everyone wanted it more than we did," she said, "and that we tried to force it for too long. The way we broke up so frequently should have been a sign."

"I still should have done better," Cole said. "I shouldn't have lost my temper and let you run off into his arms."

"And I shouldn't have made you be the one to break up with me. I should've had the courage to do it myself."

"You wanted to break up?"

"I'd already known for a long time that we were over, but I feared I'd cave to the hints from others, and go back to you again. I let others determine my actions for a long time for fear of..." Her shoulders lifted and her chin jutted out. "I ran to Heath so I wouldn't run back to you."

Cole rubbed the heel of his hand across his chest, working out the tension in his muscles. He hated that she felt she'd had to run away from him in order to start over.

"You know," she said thoughtfully, "if you had done all that you wished you had, and I had been strong enough to do all that I had wanted... then I wouldn't have Kurt. I wouldn't have Brant." She smiled through damp eyes, that ray of happiness shining once again. "I wouldn't have this tremendous love and stability in my life."

Cole nodded, understanding. "Still, I'm sorry."

"So am I," she said softly. "And I hope you're doing okay." Her eyes had dropped to the vest he was wearing.

"I am."

"Are you, though?" She raised her head and stared at him.

"Yeah."

"I mucked things up for you here." Her eyes dampened again, and Cole froze.

"No, you didn't."

"Don't lie to me!" Her anger was sudden, reminding him of the emotional storms they used to endure. "I caused you to miss out on years with your family. Your community."

"April… You weren't the only one I fought with before I left town, you know."

"I asked for space, not for you to leave."

"I know. My dad did."

He heard her gasp, then release a lengthy exhale. She looked away, then back at him as though reaffirming that he wasn't joking.

"We did a number on each other," she whispered, "didn't we?"

"We were young. Best to get our mistakes made early, right?"

She laughed, and they were silent for a long moment.

"What can I do to help?" she asked.

"Help?"

"Yes. Help you return to your rightful place back in the heart of this family and community."

"I'm working on it."

"If there's anything I can do…"

"Be a friend to Jackie."

Her eyes narrowed as though suspicious.

"I think she's going through some things," he said carefully.

"Like the whirlwind of dating you?" There was a twinkle of amusement in April's eyes, the suspicion gone.

"No. She just needs… people."

"You know we fought the night of your party. That's not a Jackie thing to do."

"What did you fight about?"

"You." April's eyes twinkled again.

"Me?"

"I told her she should kiss you."

"And she didn't think that was a good idea?" he asked, more curious than was safe.

"She didn't want a fling, and yet here the two of you are." April gave him an intrigued look, one he ignored.

"It's not a fling."

"So you two are looking at marriage?"

"No, it's not like that."

"Then what is it like?"

April's tone told him she was very much being Jackie's protective friend at the moment. Which was good. It was what he wanted. And yet he was still grateful—possibly for the first time in his life—to see his great-uncle Henry pull up.

"Something in between," he muttered. "Sorry, gotta help unload the stallion." He tipped his hat and headed toward his uncle's truck and borrowed horse trailer.

"We're not done talking about this," April called.

"Talking about my girlfriend is now officially off-limits."

"Treat her right or I'll be forced to give you a knuckle sandwich, Cole!"

He nodded, then shook his head, glancing over his shoulder to watch April retreat to the stable.

"I heard about the two of you," said a voice hardened with age.

"Hello, Uncle Henry," Cole said. "I prepared the stall for the stallion. Need help unloading?" He really didn't need another hint from someone that April was moving on.

"Jackie's a nice girl."

"I know she is." Cole was instantly wary. He clasped the back of his neck with his right hand, wondering if he could refrain from telling his uncle to mind his own business, because he was no doubt going to lay into him about dating Jackie.

"So you thought you'd mess up her life?"

"No, sir."

"She's as sassy as a summer day is long, but she doesn't have much for family. You hear what I'm saying?" Seeing Cole's hesitation, Henry lowered his voice. "Her father's forgotten who most everyone is, and her mother passed a few years ago. There's a reason she's at the Wylder dinner table on holidays, and it's not because she's pining away for you. That was nothing but a distraction, a smokescreen for what she really wants."

"What's that?" Cole held his breath, afraid his uncle wouldn't answer.

"Jackie will tell you eight ways to Sunday she's fine, but she's on the thin edge of things." Henry inhaled through his nose, then sighed as if he was carrying a great burden. "It's not my business, but I thought you should know before you carry on as if she's as strong as she looks. This family is all she's got right now."

So she wanted family? His family?

Cole met his uncle's eyes. For an old curmudgeon, he wasn't so bad, his caring side lending a welcome insight. "I appreciate the heads-up."

He'd ensure that when they broke up she was blameless.

He paused for a second, a small thought whispering through his mind that if he wasn't careful, he'd end up leaving the family ranch to give another ex "space."

"Don't run off when things go south with this one," Henry said, getting in one more lick, as was his habit. "We're honorable men."

"Things won't go south," Cole said tersely, his patience gone. "And as for leaving town when I did? I left because I was asked to." He lifted his head. "I did the honorable thing, and I'm sorry to see you've judged me negatively for listening to my family's wishes."

He turned, leaving Henry opening and closing his mouth like a Guadalupe bass trapped in the bottom of a fishing boat.

* * *

"I think I'll move to San Antonio," Jackie said, joining Cole at the edge of the riding ring. Reaching him, she balanced a clipboard on top of a nearby post.

He jolted as if in surprise, the paintbrush in his hand jerking. Panting beside her was the ranch's growing menagerie of dogs, which had barked when she'd come around the side of the stable.

"Didn't hear me come up?" she asked, amused by the way she'd caught Cole off guard. The last rain shower had ended, leaving the morning air fresh. "And isn't it too damp to be staining the new boards?"

He shrugged, displaying his work, which looked unaffected. "San Antonio? Are the rumors about us already that bad?"

"I'm sure gums are flapping around town," she said matter-of-factly.

Cole was studying her with that patient look of his, and she struggled to regain her cheerful facade.

The truth was she needed to get serious about moving her father to a facility with more dedicated memory care. And that meant the city, since there was nothing local. She wanted to be close to him, which meant she'd be moving, too. Possibly a full month before the end of her and Cole's fake romance.

"But no, I haven't *heard* any rumors," she said, gazing thoughtfully at the horse and rider being guided around the ring by Betty, the stable manager. The child was beaming, and waved excitedly as they passed.

Cole leaned against the fence, casually taking her in, and Jackie returned the favor. He was in a dirty pair of jeans and a thick plaid vest, his black hat low on his brow. He looked troubled and handsome. Her favorite combination.

"Then why would you move?" He watched her, his attention on her mouth, and she wasn't sure if he was waiting for her to say something more or if he was thinking about kissing her. She hoped the latter.

"Do you think we're stirring up a lot of gossip?" She hitched an elbow on the top board of the fence and turned to face him, resting her head against her hand. She hadn't seen him since Valentine's Day. Not even a text. It was weird being in an almost-relationship, as their roles were so undefined. She wasn't even sure how she was supposed to act with him. "You'd think people wouldn't really care what we do, since neither of us is marriage-track material."

"April read me the riot act about being good to you."

"Well, of course she did. I'm her friend and you're basically the devil."

"Ouch."

"Is she okay with us…"

"Dating?"

"Yeah."

He shrugged. "Yeah, unless I act like a jerk. Then she threatened to punch me."

"Good."

April had told her to go for it with Cole, but Jackie still feared her friend had been lying. Not that what she and Cole were doing was real, but April didn't know that, and Jackie didn't want to lose a friend over something that would go nowhere.

Cole took a step closer. Almost automatically she tipped up her chin, ready to kiss him.

"So the two of you are okay?"

A shadow crossed his face. "We worked through some things."

He slipped his arms around Jackie's waist and drew her into a hug, causing Myles's dog, Buckey, to bark playfully. Jackie leaned her head against Cole's shoulder, inhaling the scents of hay and man. The hug felt nice.

"Are you all right?" he asked.

She laughed, feeling nervous. "Why?" She slid her arms up between them, and when he didn't release her, clamped her fingers on a shirt button, exposed through his partially done up vest.

"You can tell me anything."

She lifted her gaze to his. When his expression grew solemn, full of caring and concern, she let out a shaky breath, unexpected emotion welling up inside her.

"Anything?" She gave him a playful look.

"Anything."

She batted her lashes. "You're very handsome."

He unwound one arm from around her slender waist, hooking a finger under her chin and gently lifting it so he could see her better. "I'm not going anywhere."

"Well, I might."

The arm around her waist tightened.

"Are you going to kiss me?" Anything would be better than pouring out her sorrows, because she feared Cole's kindness might melt her into a puddle. She needed to remain strong.

With torturous patience, Cole lowered his lips to hers and she kissed him.

"That's better," she said.

"Aren't you supposed to be at work?" he asked, when they broke apart after their second kiss, her body feeling tingly and warm.

"I don't know. What day is it?"

"Friday."

"Oh, right." She blinked away the haze from the kiss. She'd come here for work and had become distracted by the fine sight of a cowboy working on the riding ring's fence.

She reached for the clipboard she'd left on the fence post. "I came to talk to Levi, but your mom said he's out with a herd. So she said I could talk to you or Hank, or that new guy, Owen."

Jackie gave Cole a bright smile. "I chose you. And not just because I saw you first."

"Owen and Hank are out with the herd, too."

"Which explains why I found *you*."

"So you were bored at work and decided to stop by, to act mysterious and wheedle kisses from me?"

Their eyes met again, and she looked away as she fought a grin. She waved the clipboard stacked with white pages. "I'm an open book."

Cole snorted.

"What?" She dared him to argue.

He dutifully shook his head, mouth closed.

Good boy.

"The feed store's supplying supplements for part of the split testing in the college's cattle breeding study Brant's working on, so I came to find out what you have on hand." She gave Cole a sly look that stirred his blood. "I could have called, but you know..." She winked. "Sometimes real life visits are more fun."

He chuckled, and drank her in slowly, dropping his voice to a friendly growl. "Indeed?"

She relaxed, knowing he wasn't going to dive into personal territory such as the mess her father's life was in and how she felt about it. She was safe. He wasn't going to dive into her life and emotions like he was a real boyfriend.

* * *

Cole was feeling frustrated. Partly because he couldn't find the mineral supplements in the spot they'd once kept them, but mostly because of the way Jackie kept shutting him down. She kept locking him out of her life as if he was her fake boyfriend.

And yeah, he was. But he wanted to believe he was at least a friend that she could talk to. He'd done a good job of listening to

April's woes the other week, so why couldn't Jackie trust him with her worries like he had with her?

Cole shoved an open bag of feed aside. Their digging around in the stable's storage room was stirring up dust and making her sneeze. Not to mention how her sexy black cowboy boots with the white stitching were looking after trekking across the dirt floors.

"Doesn't Levi just let the to-be-bred herd graze on the rye he planted in the far west corner?" she asked. "I haven't heard him talk about supplements."

Cole straightened, adjusted his hat and dropped his hands on his hips. He sighed in defeat. "Shoot, Jackie. I'm sorry. I'm sadly out of touch with the ranch's details. We used to keep phosphorous in here, as well as breeding records." He'd been confident he'd find something for her, but so far was striking out and looking like an idiot who didn't know his own family's business.

Her expression softened. "I thought Levi was happy to have you back, helping."

"You'd think." Cole toed another bag out of his way, knowing he wouldn't find what he needed on the shelf behind it due to the thick layer of dust. Jackie tossed her clipboard onto one of the large white feed bags, which weighed more than she did. She pulled her phone from her back pocket and sent a text to someone.

Cole scratched his neck. Brant and April were supposed to be straightening out the records. Maybe they'd decided this dusty old room wasn't the place for them, and had moved everything to the office in the house.

Jackie performed another adorable sneeze, then reclaimed her clipboard and said, "Let's get out of here before my nose is stuffed up for the rest of day."

"Levi's been traveling a lot with Laura," he muttered. "We haven't had a chance to connect on everything yet."

"Hong Kong last week, right?"

He nodded.

The couple had spent eight days visiting Laura's sister, Ava Ross, who was scouting a location for a music video, since the sisters had missed seeing each other at Christmas. There may have been a meeting or two for Laura's new perfume business, as well.

"I'm losing track on where those two are and if they're coming or going," Jackie said, and Cole appreciated the way she was trying to make him feel better.

"Let's check the house," he said, guiding her from the room.

"I never saw Levi as someone to go traipsing across the world, and here he is, filling his passport with stamps," Jackie stated. "I took Laura to the football game and matched her up with him, you know."

"Your semi-famous matchmaking skills I've been hearing about?"

She nodded.

"You did some matchmaking with all of my brothers at games last season?"

"I did." She was wearing dark jeans and a thick black vest that brought out the pretty rose color in her cheeks. Her boots were town ones, too fancy for ranch work, sexy and somehow so Jackie. "If you want, I can take you to a game after we're done with our little thing." She gave him a wink, and he felt a strong sense of despair, as though being pulled into something that might break him.

"Anyway," she said, tucking her clipboard against her chest, "I need to get back to work. It was nice kissing you." There was that smile he adored again. Sweet and slightly devious, and able to increase his heart rate in an instant.

"Always my pleasure," he said, delighted with how his low growl made her bite her bottom lip, lift up onto her toes and plant a kiss on his lips.

Things might not be working out today with fitting back into the ranch, helping Jackie or convincing her to let him in, but the kisses were worth it.

* * *

"Hang on, I have an idea." Cole was already marching out of the stable and toward the house before Jackie could react. He paused when she reached the stable door. "You coming?"

She nodded and followed. It wasn't an unpleasant view. His jeans snugged his back end, and he was still as fit as when he'd competed in the rodeo in his twenties. He had filled out before he left town, but his build was different now, displaying more strength and power.

Though he still walked like a cowboy. She would bet his lower back was stiff every time he stood up.

They entered the house through the patio door, Buckey and Carly's sheepdog, Sergeant Riggs, following them to the threshold. "Go on now, you two. You can't come in here. You're all muddy," Cole told them.

Buckey whined, but Sergeant Riggs, as though understanding, turned and headed toward the holly hedge that separated Carly's ranch from Sweet Meadows.

The kitchen was empty and warm, scented with cinnamon. Jackie's stomach rumbled as she and Cole ditched their muddy footwear, using the wooden boot horn at the door to pry them off.

"Lunch?" Jackie asked hopefully, spying cooling trays of cinnamon buns and two apple pies alongside her BFF, lasagna, on the kitchen counter. She inhaled deeply, savoring the aromas of spicy sauces and sweetness.

Cole shook his head, a man on a mission. Jackie convinced herself to follow the soft padding of his feet and not pause to sneak a bite of Maria's delicious food.

He turned left, heading down the hallway that ran between

the sunken living room and the bedrooms. Her heart lifted when he opened the door to his room. She hurried after him and held her breath, partly in anticipation and partly to brace herself in case there were still reminders of him and April from when they'd been an off-and-on couple throughout their twenties. But as the door swung open, she noted that the room didn't even have a bed. It was cluttered with a paper-covered desk and bookshelves filled with binders, and in much more disarray than she'd expected in the typically neat home.

"What's this?" she asked from the doorway.

"Levi turned my room into an office," Cole said, his jaw clamping shut.

"Then where are you staying?"

"Down the hall."

She peeked down the hallway at the closed bedroom doors, then back at the dust that covered the office shelves, the binders with loose pages shoved into them. Stacks of books and folders, spiral-bound booklets from the county, unopened mail and piles of catalogs covered the floor.

"Are you sure Levi's in charge of this room?"

"It's a bit shocking, isn't it?" Cole said from behind the desk. He was digging through papers, clearly searching for something. "Mom keeps threatening to clean it up, but he fights it every time."

"It's a good thing you came home when you did," Jackie said as she surveyed the room. Levi was typically so anal about details. The office told a story that spoke to the true state of things on the ranch, and how overwhelmed Levi must have been with running things.

"Why's that?" Cole asked, peering at her with his bright blue eyes.

She gestured to the chaos. "He obviously needs help."

Cole scanned the room with an encompassing look, then with a sigh, opened a binder and started flipping pages. Moments later he set it down again and began moving stacks of papers on the desk, placing them back where he'd found them.

"If Laura hadn't come along he'd be completely unbearable," Jackie commented.

Cole didn't lift his head. "Why?"

"You know. Firstborn trying to rule the world. Or in this case, the ranch. Stressing out that he was going to lose the entire operation and let the family down. Your dad has very high expectations of him, doesn't he?"

"Of all of us," Cole muttered, continuing his search. The brim of his hat hid his expression, but Jackie had a feeling it was tight, with emotion held barely in-check.

"He missed you." She was wading into uncharted waters, certain there were hazards everywhere she might wander.

"My dad? I doubt that."

"He did. But Levi especially."

Cole shifted his attention to the bookshelf, attacking more binders, pulling them out, flipping them open before shoving them back into place. She caught his eyes, dark and stormy, not their usual blue.

"I'll talk to Levi about the study's details later," she said. "Really, there's no need to ransack the place."

Cole squeezed the navy blue binder in his grip, his shoulders flexing. "I want to help."

There was sorrow in his voice and Jackie sank into the chair near the door, disturbing a collection of ball caps. "Cole..."

The binder protested his tight grip, making a strangled squeaking noise before the metal rings bent with a pop. He tossed it onto a pile on the desk, sending things sliding. "Why am I even here?"

"What do you mean?"

"I'll never fit back into this world."

"It'll take time."

"I did what April needed me to do, and I let everybody else down in the process. That's not easy to fix."

"Sometimes we have to do the hard stuff for our family," she said, fidgeting with her chipped nail polish. Her Valentine's Day manicure hadn't lasted long. She should remove it, but somehow couldn't summon the energy to care. "Even if it's not what we want to do, or even what's best for us."

When she looked up Cole was watching her, the muscles in his jaw flexing.

She got up, moved to him and wrapped her arms around him, letting him know he wasn't alone, and that she understood.

"Maybe this is why people start their own families." He curved his body around her, his breath soft in her hair. "It's like a giant do-over."

* * *

"Are you really going to leave me?" Cole asked, feeling as though her comment about San Antonio had a ring of truth, a ring of sorrow.

Jackie tipped her head back, still in his arms. In those blue-and-amber-flecked irises he saw pain and worry, loss and uncertainty. He instantly wanted to make it better even though he didn't know how. He wanted to hold her tighter, not let go.

"I don't know yet." She shifted, and he reluctantly released her. "But I may not be in town until the end of May."

"A job offer?" No, it was her father. Cole could see it in the way she pulled in, closed off to protect herself. "Your dad?"

She wouldn't look at him. "He needs a level of care that isn't available locally."

"And you want to be close to him." Cole understood that, understood why she'd hugged him when they'd started talking about doing hard things for family. He'd thought the embrace was for him, but maybe she'd been the one in need. His uncle's earlier words about Jackie needing the Wylders came to mind.

She was watching him now as though expecting him to do something. It was so similar to the look April had given him when they broke up. It was a do-something, say-something, make-it-better-again look. But there was nothing he could do. Nothing to say.

"I'm sorry."

Jackie sighed and nodded.

"Hey." He reached out, gently taking her arm when she moved away, turning her to face him. "Sometimes you need to let things simmer in the back of your mind for a while. The answer will come in a flash, and then you'll strike."

"I've been doing that for months, and my dad almost got hurt as a result." Her nostrils flared, and Cole almost crossed his arms defensively before he realized she was mad at herself, not him.

"Is he okay? Like, right now?" Cole had money saved up, and maybe he could help her get through this moment.

"I don't know anymore." She collapsed on the chair with the hats again, this time sitting on the bulk of them. Her eyes welled; her shoulders slumped. She looked exhausted.

"Come here." He clasped her hand and pulled her up, then led her down the hallway to his bedroom, careful not to catch the attention of anyone who might be home.

"Cole..." She hesitated on the threshold and he gave her hand another soft tug.

"Trust me."

He closed the bedroom door behind them and pulled back the blankets on his bed.

"I should be at work."

"We'll talk about cattle feed and supplements. I promise."

She let out a snort of laughter, but climbed onto the mattress. Cole followed her, snugging his body behind hers, wrapping his arms around her, holding her close.

She was rigid at first, boxing in whatever was bothering her. He gently kissed her cheek and idly danced the tips of his fingers up and down her back, marveling at her soft curves. A woman's figure was worthy of worship. And in particular, Jackie's.

Eventually she made a contented sound and snuggled closer, relaxing. Her breathing evened out and she drifted off for a moment or two. When she stirred, he wrapped her tight in his arms, wishing to give her a longer moment of peace. But he could sense her mind was still moving, her body tightening incrementally as worry took over.

"You're going to give yourself an ulcer." When she flipped onto her back with a sigh, he propped his head on his hand and looked at her. "You okay?"

"Never better."

"You don't trust me."

She shifted to face him, flattening a palm on his pectorals. "I do."

"You don't."

"Maybe I don't trust myself."

"With me?"

"With..." Her eyes filled with tears again.

"Let me help." He drew his free hand down her arm, and when she shivered, tugged a blanket up to her shoulders.

"What's bugging you?" he asked, figuring he had a fifty-fifty chance of receiving an answer.

She shrugged, her expression clouding.

"I'm here if you want to talk." He lowered his head to the pillows and allowed his eyes to drift closed. "I'm also here if you don't want to talk." He opened one eye again and was rewarded with a smile that made him feel as though for the first time in a very long while he was with the right person. Even if he couldn't help her in the way he wanted to.

"If you want to talk about how fabulous we are together, or how you still taste like coffee, I'm here for you, Jackie." He locked his eyes on hers, letting her know that he was indeed here, even if he joked about it.

With her chin still resting on his chest, she grew quiet for a long moment. Finally she said, "I'm worried about my dad."

He watched her, listening.

"He's in a nursing home and he wandered out on Valentine's Day. He doesn't always remember where he is, or what's going on." She gave a shudder. "He almost got hit by a car."

Cole shifted to face Jackie more fully and cradled her in his arms. He brushed a strand of golden hair from her cheek, then cupped her shoulder with a hand. No wonder she'd been so tense and removed when they'd gone to the Valentine's Day dinner. She'd been holding this all inside.

"Is he okay?"

She bit her bottom lip and nodded, her eyes damp. "Someone recognized him," she said, her voice wobbling. "They brought him back, but his doctor is recommending I move him somewhere that's better equipped to deal with the pace of his progression."

Cole mulled over the implications, easing back so he could see her expression. "Would that be expensive?"

Jackie's mouth had folded into a frown. Those lips were irresistible, and he found himself moving closer so he could steal a kiss when the next opportunity arose.

She sighed. "And even farther away from Sweetheart Creek than Riverbend."

San Antonio. Her jokes had been hints about what was really going on, about what was hiding under her sunny disposition. The shadows were real.

Somehow the knowledge that she was hurting weighed more heavily than ever.

"What are you going to do?"

Her eyes clouded. "He has a bit of money left from the sale of his house, but not a lot."

"What does your brother say?"

"He's busy with his family and says whatever I decide is fine with him." Her tone was hard and Cole considered how things must be between her and her only sibling at the moment. Cole had always been able to discuss things with Levi, hash out ideas until they came up with a solution. She probably felt the same way Levi had when Cole left. The pressure to make the correct decision, to not negatively impact someone else's future, must be great.

Cole's stomach twisted as he focused on Jackie and her problem. He wanted to solve it for her, but recalled how much April had hated it when he'd tried to do that for her. He'd learned over the years that sometimes a woman just wanted you to listen, not step in and solve everything your way. Especially not without consultation. Unless it was something like changing a flat tire or opening a stuck jar lid—then it seemed to be a case of be-my-guest.

"If I move my dad into a new facility too soon, there won't be enough money left for when he really needs it. Memory care facilities can be very expensive."

"He's not well enough to be at home right now?" Cole asked.

"I couldn't do it all," she said, her voice sounding so small, so lost and hurt, full of failure. "We both needed more than a few hours of respite care, and he couldn't be left alone any longer."

"Oh, Jackie." He stroked her hair while she broke down and cried, her tears melting through his shirt, warm at first, then cooling.

He held her, wondering how he could help this woman who had in such a short time become so dear to him. He feared the only way to be of help would be to load her belongings into the back of his truck and drive her to San Antonio. And that idea made him inexplicably grumpy.

8

Cole knocked on Jackie's apartment door later that evening. When she didn't answer immediately, he knocked again, louder and more insistently. Her car was out back, but that didn't mean she hadn't walked somewhere. Instinct told him she was home.

The door opposite Jackie's opened.

"She dead or somethin'?" It was Wade Ross, scratching his potbelly with a belch that made Cole cringe. Jackie had filled him in on Wade's story. Apparently the man had lost his family's eighty-year-old business as well as his wife in one short month, sending him into a tailspin. It was shocking how a few strokes of bad luck could change a man so quickly.

Cole turned back to the door and knocked again. "I'm taking my girlfriend out for a date." It was Friday, and they had a fake relationship to uphold, after all.

"Keep your pants on," Jackie complained from inside the apartment. Cole heard the flick of the dead bolt and the door opened. A small smile played on her lips. "In your case, that expression doesn't apply. You're welcome to take your pants off anytime, anyplace."

"Don't keep me up all night. We share a wall." Wade pointed at the wall dividing the two apartments, gave Cole a dirty look and slammed his door.

Goose, with his pink tongue lolling lazily to the left, ambled up to Jackie and sat heavily beside her feet. Music started up in Wade's apartment, and the dog slid onto his belly with a moan, chin resting on his paws.

Jackie grinned, but Cole's mind was stuck on what she'd said earlier. "Any place?"

"I'm sure Sheriff Johnson would understand if he caught you without pants."

Cole shuddered at the prospect of public indecency.

Jackie stepped aside to let him into her apartment, her dog trotting over to the couch, claiming it as his. Cole caught a whiff of strawberries as he passed Jackie, and backtracked a step, leaning in to place a kiss on her lips. He meant for it to be short and sweet, but as usual, it deepened, pulling him in. He shifted his weight, bringing her into his arms.

"That's better," she said as they broke apart. The sweet look of pleasure that brightened her face made his heart feel lighter than it had all day. Though he'd been sorely out of place since returning home, right now, with Jackie in his arms, everything seemed right.

"Are you busy?" He bumped his nose against hers.

"I might be able to clear my schedule."

"Put on your dancing shoes."

"Why?"

"I figure if you're moving to the city, we need to make the most of our time together in Sweetheart Creek." He brushed a thumb over her cheek as sorrow replaced their earlier happiness.

She didn't want to go.

The feeling was mutual.

"Very logical," she said smoothly. "I'll find my shoes."

"The town will be boring without you," he said, pulling her in for another kiss, to let her know it was true.

"Good thing it's not a long drive," she said. "I can still come and instigate fun."

"Well?" He didn't release his grip on her. "Are you going to put on your dancing shoes or what?"

She smirked. "Maybe if you let me go."

"Never." He angled his head, kissing her again. As soon as her lips touched his, he was gone. All thought and all worries left, and nothing remained but himself and Jackie. As the kiss deepened, he braced them with a hand against the doorjamb. They were either going to have to move inside or get onto that dance floor.

When they broke free, he dropped his arms, allowing Jackie to drift away enough that she could drink him in. She grinned and dragged a finger down the line of snap buttons on his shirt. "I see you put some effort in again tonight. Very handsome." She hooked a finger around the snap near his belly button and gave a tug. The clasp held, and her smile became slightly more wicked. She edged her feet between his, bringing her other hand to the snap and pulling it apart with a quiet click. She watched him as she moved to the next snap. Then the next.

"Undressing me won't help."

"Help what?" she asked.

He didn't want to think about his reputation, or hers, or anything but the way her mouth felt on his right now.

He duck-walked them into the apartment, shutting the door. He pressed her against it and continued to kiss her. She gave a low growl of satisfaction as he pulled her shirt from the waist of her jeans.

There was more of a softness to Jackie this evening. Cole couldn't put his finger on it other than her mood was less desperate, less fiery, and more of a slow burn seated in a deeper need. He didn't need to understand it to know it felt natural and more meaningful than any other moment they'd shared so far.

He gently caressed her ear with his thumb as they kissed, angling his head for better access to her mouth. Her tongue, wet and hot, met his and he pulled off his hat, tossing it off to the side, not caring where it landed.

But things didn't get wild and crazy like he'd expected. Their kisses and caresses continued to intensify slowly, leaving him even more desperate for her. All of her. Everything from reveling in the small things, like the feel of her skin under his callused fingers, to the softness of her nape, the firmness of her jawbone, the way her hair entangled his fingers, falling forward to curtain them on one side. She smelled of fruit and something so Jackie that he knew he would never smell it on anyone but her.

The kisses felt more intimate than anything he'd ever experienced, and the two of them were still fully clothed, still standing.

It was then, and without a doubt, that he realized if Jackie left town, he would follow.

* * *

Kissing Cole was so beautiful Jackie wanted to cry. She clutched the front of his shirt in a fist and lowered her forehead to his collarbone to catch her breath. This felt like so much more than a fake relationship.

She tipped her head up, trying to decipher how Cole was feeling. Judging by the glazed look in his eyes, he was as lost in the moment as she was.

He cupped her face with so much tenderness that she caught her breath, and he angled in, giving her a sweet, soft kiss that made her feel so loved and cared for it left her fighting tears again.

When Cole's feet bracketed hers, like they did now, she felt sheltered, and as though everything would be all right.

His lips ran a line of light kisses up the bridge of her nose and across her forehead, worshiping and cherishing her. It was sensual and so unlike any of their other kisses.

"What are we doing?" she whispered.

He grunted something indecipherable and scooped her up in his arms, his cowboy boots echoing across her wood floors before he kicked open her bedroom door and gently laid her on her bed. "I thought we'd go dancing, but I believe our plans have changed."

Instead of peeling off her clothes, Cole climbed onto the bed beside her and pulled her against him. He was sheltering her, giving her what he felt she needed as he had earlier in the day. Knowing she needed someone to hold on to even though she'd refused to let him in.

But she had. She'd let him in back at the ranch, told him her worries, released them. It had been freeing, exhausting, and it left her feeling hollow, yet less alone.

As she grew sleepy in Cole's safe warm embrace, he continued trailing slow kisses, and when she woke up in the shelter of his arms the next morning, he was still there, watching her.

Yesterday's painful feelings of being alone, lost and broken, had waned. Today she felt as though she could tackle the world again, and as though life wasn't so bad, after all.

"Thanks for staying," she said, as Goose jumped up onto the bed and dropped himself over her feet.

"Anytime," Cole said, his voice gravelly with sleep. He rolled onto his back, smiling at the ceiling, eyes closed, his five o'clock shadow adding to his rugged appeal. A tuft of dark hair stuck up on the side that hadn't been resting on the pillow. They were still cuddled close, his shirt snaps open, revealing the white T-shirt he wore underneath. She ran a hand through the gap in his plaid shirt, absorbing the warmth and strength of his body.

"I like Saturday mornings," she said, realizing there was no rush, nothing to pull her away to face the day.

"Me, too," he said, deepening what started as a light kiss and segued into something with serious heat.

Jackie peeled his shirt upward and tossed it on the floor. Her own shirt quickly joined it.

"Are you sure?" Cole asked, such tenderness in his voice that Jackie hesitated, wondering if she was making a mistake. Wondering if she was going to fall the rest of the way out of this crush and into something that could only be defined as love.

* * *

Jackie was wrapped in his arms, her bedroom smelling uniquely, deliciously of her. As they cuddled, slowly allowing their heart rates to calm, Cole settled into that pleasant place between intense satisfaction and sleep. His body felt relaxed, spent, content. Happy.

The tender, giving moments between them last night, as well as this morning, had been a lot different from anything they'd shared in the past.

And soon she'd be leaving town. Leaving him.

He wanted to follow her, but wasn't sure she'd allow it.

None of this felt fake any longer. Not for him. And the idea that it might be one-sided left him feeling choked up.

He sighed, burrowing his face in Jackie's soft hair, refusing to think about the future. They had now. Right now.

"I heard you coughing in your sleep," he said. "You should probably stay in bed."

"I wasn't coughing!" Jackie rolled over so she could drape herself across Cole's chest.

"That's too bad."

She checked the time with a frown. "Don't you have chores?"

"I texted Myles. He's got them."

Jackie sat up. "He doesn't mind?"

The brothers had always agreed that the five of them should

have a life outside the ranch, and that when needed, the others would step in and help out. He sort of owed his brothers a few years' worth of missed chores, but being here with Jackie felt important, and he knew Myles, who was deeply in love with Karen, would understand.

Jackie was letting Cole in, letting him help her, and he was glad she'd allowed him to stay. He felt less alone and lost around her. Like he was part of something. Which meant he needed to figure out how to get Jackie to stay in Sweetheart Creek.

She slipped out of bed, went to her dresser, pulling together an outfit.

"What are you doing?" he asked.

"Getting dressed." She tucked the clothes under an arm. He had a feeling she knew that if she didn't leave her bed now, she might not do so until Monday morning. "So we go dancing tonight, since we missed out last night?"

"All of my evenings are free," he said meaningfully. He was happy to fill them with Jackie. Whether they were mowing grass for Mrs. Fisher or right here in her bed didn't matter, as long as he was with her.

Her lips lifted in a smile, as though she liked the implication that he might keep himself available for her—and not just as part of their fake relationship. It warmed his heart more than he wanted to admit.

* * *

Jackie stumbled out of her apartment with Cole, smiling into the sunshine, her hand linked with his. There was a cool morning breeze, and the hearts and red streamers in the window of the Big Hair salon had been replaced with shamrocks, despite St. Patrick's Day being several weeks away.

She'd made love with Cole that morning, and it had been

heavenly. Better than anything, ever. There'd been a connection, a link… Exhilarating.

She beamed at him, and he tightened his hand around hers as they walked toward the diner, shoulders rubbing.

"What's wrong with Bill?" Jackie asked, stopping when they reached the foot-wide gap between Big Hair and the electronics store. The well-known armadillo, the tormentor of Sweetheart Creek, was curled in a ball between the buildings.

"Is he hurt?" Cole slowed to a stop. He dropped a kiss on Jackie's temple, and she warmed from the tips of her toes to her nose.

He glanced down the sidewalk, then back at the armadillo. "I'll ask Brant." Cole snapped a photo of the mammal and sent it to his brother.

"What does he say?" Jackie asked, still watching Bill. She liked being exactly where she was, leaning lightly against Cole, in no hurry to be anywhere else.

"Don't know yet."

"Call him."

Cole hesitated, then said, "It's calving season. He's going to be extra tired and ornery."

"Are we still talking about Brant?" Jackie asked. "Or did we switch back to Bill?"

"Still Brant." Cole chuckled, kissing her again. It seemed he couldn't get enough, just like her. She was tempted to pull him back to her apartment.

"April's used to his sweet side. She'll be in for a surprise." As a vet, he spent a lot of late nights out in the boonies, helping calving situations that had gone wrong.

"Nah, she saw us at our worst while growing up alongside us on the ranch."

"Is it okay they're together now?" Jackie had asked him that before, but he'd never actually replied. She'd basically been avoiding April, afraid what her friend might say about her moving in on April's ex. Even if it was fake.

Because it wasn't.

Definitely not.

Not anymore.

Moving to San Antonio sure was going to hurt.

"Of course. Everyone's moved on." Cole waved his silent phone, then pocketed it. "He must be out on a call."

"Cole?"

He turned to Jackie, meeting her eyes. "We've all moved on."

She watched him for a long moment, trying to find a sliver of doubt, a lie, anything to tell her that he was still hung up on his ex, and therefore off-limits.

Safe to crush on because she could never ever have him.

She could find nothing, and a shiver of fear rippled up her spine.

He was hers to claim.

9

Cole kissed Jackie there on Main Street again, trying to parlay that he had absolutely no designs on anyone but her. When they pulled apart Jackie looked lost, happy and slightly dazed. There was definitely no more doubt hiding in the shadows of her eyes.

April was now with the man that Cole had always secretly believed she should choose. Maybe that was part of the reason things hadn't worked between them. He'd tried too hard to be different from Brant, to keep her away from him, to have her think his brother was boring.

Had it been sibling rivalry, jealousy, a worry that something in himself was missing? That soft, kind streak he saw in Brant and that others responded to, instantly loving him?

It didn't really matter what or why. April was where she was supposed to be, and Cole was feeling as though he was, too.

Except Jackie was leaving. That was an even bigger barrier than convincing her that something real was growing between them, underneath the facade of their fake relationship.

How could he fix it so she could stay?

"Cole?" Jackie was looking at him with an amused expression. He'd tuned out for only a second or two, but she'd noticed.

He'd wasted time being away from Sweetheart Creek, being away from Jackie. And now it was almost too late for them to figure things out and make something of this.

He huffed a breath and adjusted his hat, frustrated. "I should have come home sooner." Truly, he'd been afraid of his reception, and if Clint hadn't called him, he wasn't sure how long he would have kept roaming.

Cole moved, causing Bill to straighten from his balled position and scurry down the alley, his scales hitting the sides of the two buildings as he waddled.

"Oh!" Jackie let out a surprised squeak, no doubt having forgotten about the beast.

"Guess he's all right," Cole said, snapping a blurry photo of the armadillo running away. He sent it to Brant.

"Why *didn't* you come home sooner?" she asked.

He shrugged, unable to express his fears or pain. Even to her.

"Oh, Cole." Jackie grabbed him by the arms, her expression sympathetic, as though she'd seen his inner side. "I'm so sorry."

"I had some good adventures." He gave her a crooked grin. "It wasn't all bad. I learned a lot about myself."

But why couldn't he have come home for his dad's wedding last June when Brant had asked him to, and discovered Jackie then?

She watched him for a long moment before gesturing to the narrow tunnel the animal had escaped down. "I'm glad he's okay."

"I've heard people don't like him."

"Oh, don't get me wrong," Jackie said, her tone full of amusement as they began walking again. She pushed open the door to the Longhorn Diner and Cole grabbed it, holding it for her before following her inside. "He's a giant pain in the butt. But I couldn't imagine the town without him."

"Kind of like my uncle Henry?" Cole asked, catching sight of him in the back of the diner, spinning on his stool to see who was entering the bacon-scented building.

The man beside Henry turned as well: Cole's dad. Roy gazed at him with those familiar blue Wylder eyes.

Not wanting to have his mood spoiled by either relative, Cole snagged Jackie's elbow, directing her into a booth near the door. "Let's sit here."

He slid in across from her, and when she rested her hand on the tabletop, he linked his fingers with hers. He told himself it was to further their charade, not because he wanted to feel connected with her at all moments of his day.

"What are you going to order?" he asked.

"The ranch house special."

Bacon and eggs, toast, sausage and oatmeal, if he recalled correctly.

"You getting the Wylder special?" she asked.

"They still have that?" As teenagers, he and his brothers would often have breakfast at home, hustle through their chores, then head to school early, stopping by for a second breakfast if time permitted. During their teenage growth spurts he was pretty sure their constantly hollow stomachs had kept the diner's financials well in the black. Every day they'd order the same thing. Bacon and scrambled eggs, sourdough toast, shredded hash browns and pancakes. It had been nicknamed the Wylder special, and it surprised him people still referred to it as such.

"Laura ordered it when she came to town," Jackie said.

"That little bit of a thing? Are both her legs hollow?" Laura Oakes still had the physique of a fashion model, her former career, and it amazed him to hear she could and would consume a meal as large as the Wylder special.

"The town's goal is to get her back to human size," Jackie said with a laugh. "Although she doesn't seem to put up much of a protest. That girl likes her food. I can't imagine what it must've been like trying to stay a size zero or whatever she was while working."

"Are you talking about Laura?" Mrs. Fisher asked, coming along with her coffeepot. She filled their cups without asking, then placed cream and sugar in front of Jackie.

"I was saying how she ordered the Wylder special when she came to town."

"Oh yes," Mrs. Fisher said, beaming. "Bill gave her a fright that morning. And when she put in her order, I knew she and Levi were destined to be a couple. She even asked for extra syrup like he does." She gave a satisfied little shoulder wiggle. "I wasn't wrong."

"You don't get credit for them," Jackie protested. "I'm the one who took them to a game."

"You think you're a matchmaker," Mrs. Fisher teased with a sly smile and a twinkle in her eyes.

"I am!" Jackie said loudly, causing people to turn her way. Letting go of Cole's hand, she leaned out into the aisle and spied Davis Davies, the local radio DJ. "Aren't I? People go to a game with me and soon they're matched up with their true love. Right?"

Mrs. Fisher sucked in her cheeks as though fighting a grin.

"Yes, Jackie," Davis said impatiently. "We all know. Levi, Myles, Brant, Ryan." He gave Cole a meaningful look.

Cole raised his hands as if innocent. He'd never gone to a game with Jackie. Not technically.

"Yeah, you're a problem," Jackie said, eyeing him. "You're marring my perfect Wylder match-up streak."

"Too bad the season is over," Mrs. Fisher said. "But from what I've heard, neither of you are single, anyway." She pivoted, topping up Davis's cup with coffee.

"Want to know a secret?" Cole asked, leaning across the table. Jackie swiveled back into the booth. "I was sitting behind you at the state championship game."

There was a long moment of silence.

"You were not," Jackie said in a tiny voice.

"You were wearing leggings under a miniskirt, a white sweatshirt, and your were taking stats."

She gasped, then her eyes narrowed. "You saw me on TV."

"If you'd turned around, you would have seen me three rows up."

"No," she breathed. "Perfect score. Five for five."

"I don't think that counts," Mrs. Fisher said, turning back to their table, having obviously eavesdropped. "Can you set *yourself* up with someone? Especially if you don't know they're there?"

Jackie's attention was still on Cole. "Why *were* you there?"

"To watch the game. I've been to all of the State games."

"Why didn't you…" She grew silent and dropped her eyes. She knew why he hadn't come down to celebrate, to speak to his brothers or show his face. April had been there. And Cole had been respecting her wishes, not wanting to horn in on a celebration on-field, not ready to break the silence with his family.

Sitting in a small brew pub in Blueberry Springs, Colorado, day after day he'd mulled over the decision: go home or give everyone more time? He'd always opted to play it safe. In part, he knew, because he was afraid what he might return to. His father hadn't reached out to him at all over the years, his brother Brant being the only one making an effort. Levi had finally started calling a few months ago, but had never left more than a "'Levi here'" message that didn't give Cole anything to act upon. It had been enough to keep him away.

Mrs. Fisher cleared her throat. "My yard's looking good, and I heard that's because of y'all."

"We know nothing," Jackie and Cole said at the same time. His eyes cut to hers and she giggled.

"Um-hmm? Is that so?" the waitress asked, placing a manicured hand on her hip.

"We would never lie to you, Mrs. Fisher," Jackie said sweetly.

She harrumphed, and said, "Whatcha ordering?" She studied them both. "Judging from your expressions, you two may need to replenish your energy stores." She winked.

Jackie rolled her eyes, her face turning a deep, endearing red as she placed her order. Cole simply grinned.

Mrs. Fisher took Cole's order, giving his shoulder a squeeze as she leaned in to say, "Thank you for the yard work, hon. You're a good one."

"What did she say?" Jackie asked when she'd left.

Cole shook his head, feeling a swell of gratitude and emotion. "She doesn't believe we didn't do her yard."

"Well, half the town, along with her husband, saw us."

"I didn't do it for the attention."

"I know."

As they waited for their breakfasts, Jackie told tales about people they both knew, helping fill in backstory on things he'd missed while he was away. As he listened, he avoided thinking about how she was considering moving out of Sweetheart Creek.

It didn't feel real. She had to change her mind at some point, because he couldn't imagine her not here. Whenever someone passed their booth she gave them a bright smile and a wave, which was always returned. She belonged here.

They both looked up when someone paused beside them, and Jackie's bright smile faded. It was Cole's great-uncle, Henry Wylder.

"I thought you were smarter," Henry said to Jackie.

Cole bristled as she drew herself taller.

"She is very smart," Cole said loudly, causing his father to turn on his stool at the back counter, eyes narrowed at Henry. Cole gave a barely perceptible shake of his head and Roy slowly returned to his coffee. Cole really didn't need his dad bailing him and Jackie out of a conversation with Uncle Curmudgeon. It might turn into a fight between himself and his father instead of Cole politely putting Henry in his place while defending his girlfriend. Or himself. Because Cole bet Henry was going to come after him by the end of this little tête-à-tête.

His uncle's lips formed a stern line, no doubt feeling the town all watching from their own tables. He glowered at Cole before flicking his attention to Jackie. "Do yourself a favor and stay away from this one. He's not a man you can count on when things get tough."

Cole ground his teeth together so he wouldn't say anything his uncle, or the diner's many eavesdroppers, would find worth repeating around town.

"Oh, Henry, sweetie. You underestimate me." Jackie winked at Cole. "He's the one who should watch out for me." She waited a beat, then said coyly, looking up through her lashes, "When was the last time I kept a man longer than a month or two?" She laughed, but Cole heard the hint of pain in her light tone.

Henry's frown deepened. "It doesn't mean it's a smart match-up just because you've been chasing him since you were knee-high to a grasshopper."

"That I have," she purred. "And I finally caught him." She stroked the top of Cole's hand. Her sultry look stirred his blood.

Cole cleared his throat, but his voice came out husky as he said, "Quite willingly on my part."

Henry snorted, clearly annoyed with their act. "She had to pay to catch you by purchasing you in an auction." He gave Cole an appraising look. "She can do better."

"I know." Cole grinned at Jackie, who grinned right back.

"Don't you forget it." His uncle continued to the door, leaving. Before the other diners had a chance to turn back to their meals, Cole half raised himself from the bench, leaned over the table and captured Jackie's face in his hands. Swiftly he gave her a long, wet kiss to show the town exactly how he felt about JackieLynn Moorhouse.

* * *

On Monday morning, Jackie shuffled papers in her small office above the feed store, procrastinating on tracking down some missing receipts. She thumbed out a text to Lucy, who worked downstairs, to see if she had some on her desk. Then she stood and stared out the window that overlooked the loading area. She couldn't stop thinking about Cole and their weekend together, and how he'd been sitting just three rows behind her at the state championship football game.

Somewhere between Friday morning and now her feelings for him had developed into something pretty big, and she couldn't dodge the notion that Cole was in step with her.

Wishful thinking?

Possibly.

But Henry had pointed out the very things she had been avoiding thinking about. She had been chasing Cole since she was a kid, and what they were doing right now was just for show. Cole wasn't someone she could count on over the long haul, and she shouldn't expect to.

Yes, he would fix her bumper and show up when she needed a smile. But he wasn't going to solve the big problems in her life, and it would be ridiculous to expect that of him when they weren't an actual couple, despite how deep the two of them had dived into the charade. She was leaving town, and when he'd heard the news it was like he'd shut down emotionally and released her, as though their relationship wasn't something worth fighting for. As though what they had wasn't worth preserving. As if he still felt they were playacting, when they weren't.

Was what they had really that much different from what he and April had battled for years? He'd left town when things got sticky instead of raising his fists and fighting. Jackie understood why he'd gone, and it had likely been the right thing to do. But it also felt as though staying away for so long may have been the easy way out rather than coming back home and facing everyone again.

She sighed, her earlier elation sliding into something that resembled her old friend Mr. Glum.

She just wished she had more time to figure things out with Cole.

"Are you okay?"

Jackie snapped her head up at the sound of Lucy's voice. "Yeah, why?"

She gestured to Jackie's former slumped position, then said, "Usually you come downstairs to chat if you need something." She gave her a folder of receipts.

"Thanks."

"You sure everything's okay?" Lucy paused. "I heard you and Cole are dating?"

"We are. He's magnificent." Jackie allowed a trace of her true feelings to sound in her voice, to add credence to her words.

"I saw you walking this morning. You two are really cute together." Lucy's expression grew wistful. "I haven't smiled like you two in a very long time."

And that was the problem. Jackie was smiling like she hadn't in a very long time, too. Or maybe ever.

But it was all going to end in the most heartbreaking way, and there was nothing she could do about it.

* * *

Cole saw Jackie coming across the yard, the damp March air putting a rosy color in her cheeks as the dogs chased her, wagging their tails. He felt the beginnings of a grin and considered playing it cool, since they were technically still in a fake relationship despite things being fairly hot and heavy for the past month.

Jackie had spent the last day and a half in the city, doing some research and looking into a new care facility for her father, and Cole had missed her like crazy. His days were boring without her, and he'd taken to carrying his phone with him on the off chance she'd shoot him a text or call him.

She had a few times, and he'd been so eager to hear from her he'd nearly fumbled his beeping phone right into a horse trough full of water. He felt like a teenager, gluing his nose to the screen, tapping out messages, hearing phantom rings. Swearing he felt a vibration for a message that hadn't been sent.

Now she was here in person. And she was smiling, her pace quickening as she drew near, and his own smile won out over his pride.

He set down the brushes he'd been using to clean a saddle out in the March sunshine, and headed toward her with long-legged strides. "Hey, pretty lady. Looking for a cowboy?"

"Just one," she said, beaming at him.

Man, this felt real.

It *was* real.

He held out his arms and quickened his last steps, and Jackie leaped on him, wrapping her legs around him as if she'd missed him as much as he'd missed her.

He met her lips with a hungry kiss that went on so long his arms started to ache from holding her so tightly.

"Welcome home."

She nuzzled into the spot where his neck and chest met, and gave a sigh of contentment, then leaned back, still in his arms.

Home.

Reluctantly, he allowed her feet to slide back to the ground, but continued to hold her close. "Doing anything tonight?" he asked.

"Does my fake boyfriend have plans for me?"

Ouch. That fake stuff had to go.

"He does. And so do I."

"And so do *you*?" She was still smiling; her guard hadn't gone up at the hint that he didn't want to be fake any longer. She looked more curious than anything.

He hesitated, rethinking the wisdom of what he wanted to do. She was leaving town.

Reality.

"Dinner?" he asked, releasing her.

"When?" She pulled her phone from the back pocket of her jeans, checking the time.

"As soon as I finish cleaning this saddle?"

"I can help."

Before long he was caught up in Jackie's stories, in the way her eyes brightened when she laughed, the way he felt warmth all the way into his chest whenever their hands brushed.

"Are you even listening?" she scolded when he found himself lost in one of her smiles.

"What?"

"You're such a poor listener."

"I was listening to subtext," he suggested with a grin, knowing he'd missed the past few sentences of her story.

She gripped his chin, holding him still so she could kiss him. "And what did that subtext say?"

"You're wearing a pink bra today," he replied, sliding his arms around her waist to give her another kiss.

She groaned. "Is that all you think about?"

"No. Not always." He kissed her again with a passion that left his head spinning. He reluctantly broke the embrace when someone behind him cleared a throat.

"Is the saddle ready?" asked Betty, the riding manager. She sounded amused rather than impatient.

"Almost. I just have to ask Jackie one more thing." He lowered his lips to hers once again.

"You need to ask her what she had for lunch?" Betty teased, her tone dry. "Give me the saddle. It's good enough."

When Cole turned to glance over his shoulder the older woman was shaking her head.

"It's done," Jackie said, sliding from Cole's arms, blushing endearingly.

And so was he. Done pretending.

* * *

Jackie and Cole headed inside the ranch house through the patio door, the coolness of the rapidly approaching evening making them hustle. Jackie felt happy, alive.

She'd found a place for her father that would give him adequate care without completely breaking the bank. All she had to do was avoid thinking about moving to San Antonio and leaving her own life—and everyone in it—behind.

Cole had been holding her hand, seeming as eager to stay physically connected as she was after two days apart. She'd done her best not to bombard him with text messages while in the city, but he'd been so quick to reply she'd let herself send him her thoughts, strange sightings and whatnot. It was too easy to hope and dream, despite knowing that this was going to end in May, if not sooner.

Maria was standing at the kitchen island with her hands in sudsy water. Her smile grew as she watched Cole give Jackie a light kiss on the lips before heading past her to go get cleaned up.

"We're going out for supper. Jackie's back."

"I can see that," Maria said, pleasure lifting her voice. "How are you? Cole said you found somewhere for your dad?" She had dried her hands and came over, arms out for a hug, which felt warm and welcoming.

Jackie swallowed hard. Suddenly she saw nothing but the heartbreaking flaws in her plans for her father. When she moved, she'd be leaving her support system. Her friends might not know how bad her father was doing, and they might not know how much she needed them, but she did.

But if she found a way to stay, and things got twisted and ugly between her and Cole, she would lose this family just the same. She would lose the place that felt like home.

But even worse was knowing that when she left town as well as Cole, she could come back to visit Maria and her family, sharing meals in this kitchen. And she'd see Cole—the man she loved. Her feelings were so much stronger than a crush. And one day she might see him here with a wife and family of his own.

She shuddered in Maria's arms and the woman released her, holding her face between her warm hands, studying her for a long moment. Jackie gave her a bright smile, worried what she might see.

"Oh, honey." Maria wrapped her in a fresh hug, sending tears streaming down Jackie's cheeks.

10

Cole couldn't imagine Jackie living in any of the places they'd looked at in San Antonio that morning. None of the neighborhoods felt as though the people living there would take care of her in the way the folks in Sweetheart Creek did.

But what was she going to do? Spend three hours in the car every time she wanted to zip into the city to check on her father? Sure, it wasn't that far, but door to door, the miles and time added up.

Jackie had to leave town, her friends. Him.

Even though it was dusk, the work on the ranch done for the day, Cole headed to the riding stable, determined to do something productive, as well as get lost in a task.

Grabbing a shovel, he began cleaning out stalls so Betty wouldn't have to do it in the morning. There were other things he could do on the ranch, tasks that would take more skill, but he didn't feel as though he could step in and do them without talking to Levi first.

And yeah, he could go find his brother. He'd spotted Laura's car parked out front when he got home, and her terrier, Target, had jumped up on him with excitement when he'd entered the house. But Levi was likely busy and didn't want his time with his gal interrupted.

Cole finished cleaning out the last stall and stretched his lower back. He stood in the doorway to the stable, noting how dark it had become. Full darkness would close in soon, which meant it was probably around seven thirty.

"What are you up to?" Levi asked, joining him.

"Where's Laura?"

"She went back to her place for the night."

"That's early for her." She usually stayed until at least ten o'clock before returning to her one-bedroom rental in town.

"Did you clean out the stalls?" Levi asked, eyeing the full wheelbarrow.

Cole grunted in acknowledgment, lifting the wheelbarrow's handles to go dump the contents out back. They walked in silence, Levi at his side, carrying a pitchfork even though Cole wouldn't need it to empty his load.

"I hear Jackie's leaving," Levi stated, as Cole tipped the wheelbarrow, dumping the soiled straw onto the heap near a grove of cedars, dark shadows of the approaching night lengthening. Levi used the pitchfork to heave the straw higher on the pile.

"End of the month." Just three weeks. They had been continuing with their relationship for the past month as though everything was still normal. But each day their smiles got a little tighter, their goodbyes a little longer.

Cole waited for his brother to finish, then turned to head back to the stable.

"You'll be moving on?"

"What?" Cole's steps slowed.

"I imagine the ranch isn't so exciting after you've spent years mountain climbing and having adventures. And now with your gal leaving, there's not much to stay for."

Cole eyed his brother as they walked, his heart pounding hard in his chest. It was getting too dark to see his expression. "Is that what you want? For me to leave?"

Levi blinked under the light above the stable doors, as though he hadn't expected the question. "Well, aren't you?"

"I hadn't planned on it."

His brother frowned. "You're not going with Jackie?"

Cole shook his head as he parked the wheelbarrow at the back of the stable near the stack of fresh straw, ready for its next job. It would be presumptuous to invite himself along on her journey, certain to create a disaster out of something good.

"Why not?"

"Why should I?" Cole asked, his tone hard. She hadn't so much as hinted he might be welcome to tag along. With lengthy strides he headed back to Cookies's stall, where he'd left the shovel, and tossed it into the wheelbarrow with a clatter.

"Seemed like the two of you were serious, is all."

Cole didn't respond. He'd been hanging out with Jackie nearly every night, and while he'd started dating her to show the town and his family he'd grown up and was ready to settle down, now he actually felt that way.

And to add another pain in his heart, it was working. He'd noticed a shift. People were asking him to help with things as if he was staying in town, watering those dormant roots that had always been there.

Which would have been great except he was no longer dating Jackie to show off a different side to himself, but because he cared for her.

And she was leaving.

"I haven't noticed her with someone in a long time," Levi stated. "And maybe never like this."

Cole ground his teeth together. Things were stressful enough for her right now without him causing complications because he was feeling things for her. She could make a move, just like he could, and the ball was very much in her court.

But man, did he ever want to create complications. Desperately.

"I'm not breaking her heart, if that's what you're asking. She's leaving for her dad."

Levi lifted his hands as though calming a horse about to rear. "I didn't say you were."

"She's a good woman, Levi."

"I know." His brother sighed. "Look, I'm not trying to fight."

Cole crossed his arms and let out a long, slow breath. Levi was standing near the door now, essentially blocking it. Cole would be a jerk if he blew by him, but he wasn't loving this conversation.

"I know I haven't given you as much work around here as you might want," Levi said, his voice low and even.

"It's fine."

"No, it's not." Levi's tone became grim. "You've been trying, and I've been punishing you. At least that's what Laura says."

Smart woman.

"It's fine. Really."

"Quit lying," Levi snapped.

"I understand I broke your trust by leaving," Cole said cautiously, "and that I need to rebuild it."

"No." Levi was shaking his head. "I should have apologized to you a long time ago."

"For not working me to the bone as soon as I stepped over the threshold?" Cole said with a chuckle that sounded a bit bitter. "Don't worry about it."

"No," Levi repeated firmly. Above the wide doorway a naked bulb glowed, casting shadows that made him look even more serious than his tone suggested. "For sending you away."

Cole scoffed in surprise. "You didn't send me away."

"I acted like my solution to the problem with April was the only one possible. I didn't give you the space to figure out what was best for you. I put you in a take-it-or-leave-it situation. You left it, and we haven't spoken for years. I don't like that, and I'm ashamed I treated you that way."

Cole let his brother's apology sink in. He hadn't realized how much he'd been wanting to hear him say that.

"So you're saying you're bossy?" Cole suggested, lifting an eyebrow. His brother tipped his head down with a huff of amusement as well as an acknowledgment of the truth.

Cole's chest felt tight, and a lump of emotion seemed to be lodged in his throat. Levi had told him that he should stay, step in, take charge of April's life and make everything better. So had Brant, but in a slightly different way. It hadn't been what April had wanted, though. And afraid that revealing her wishes would cause her further judgment from the family she needed, Cole had remained silent, taking his lumps. When he'd left the next morning, no doubt Levi had felt he was to blame, as had Brant, not knowing there was so much more to the story.

"Laura's been telling me I get caught up in thinking that my way is the only way. I'm learning that's not always true."

"You didn't send me away."

"You probably could have used a brother that night. Instead of listening, I dictated what I thought was best."

"Levi, I didn't leave because of you. I left because it was what April wanted and needed." He let his brother consider that. "And trust me. Everyone in the family had similar conversations with me that night. There were a lot of opinions about what I should do, and none of them were what April wanted. She's important to this family. She's a Wylder, and not just because she married Brant. April's always been one of us, and I needed to let her have this family and this town. She was going through some tough stuff and needed the support. If I was here, it would have made it tougher. She asked for space and I agreed. She didn't ask me to leave. I did it because it was for the best."

"You stayed away a long time," Levi stated.

"And now I'm home."

"Some reception you've gotten," he said, tsking regretfully.

"I have fences to mend."

"Well, consider this one mended, because I'm truly sorry for judging you, for not supporting you and for not calling sooner."

"What was with those voice mails, anyway?" Cole asked, amused. He imitated his brother's tight tone in the messages. "'Levi here. Levi Wylder.'"

His brother laughed, his expression softening with humor. "I was trying, man." It felt as though they were back working on the corral earlier in the season. Replacing the weak boards with new ones, protecting and strengthening the fence with fresh stain so it would last for years to come.

"Well, I appreciated it." Even though he hadn't known how to respond.

"I'm not done," Levi said, growing serious again. "You're an equal partner in this ranch, and while I haven't taken the time to bring you up to speed around here, I hope to do so soon." He angled his head, watching Cole. "If you're interested."

Cole stared at him, the question hanging in the air. Should he stay? Did he want this life? And could his brother trust him to have his back once again?

The answer to all those questions was yes.

Cole stepped forward and gripped Levi's hand firmly. "You can count on me, big bro."

* * *

Jackie sat across from Cole at a small table in The Watering Hole, the end of April only two weeks away. They were both drinking whiskey, which was a direct result of Cole betting Jackie she couldn't pull off wearing a pink feather boa around town. Or wouldn't want to. She had, and so now they had glasses of dirt-cheap whiskey sitting in front of them, and were making funny faces over every sip.

"Thanks for helping Mrs. Fisher back in February and then again this month," Travis Nestner said, giving Cole a pat on the back. The mayor caught Daisy-Mae as she hustled past, filling in as a server. "Their next round is on me." She nodded and carried on.

"Man, we should switch to the good stuff," Cole told Jackie.

"Don't you dare," Travis said.

Cole chuckled. He and Jackie had helped the Fishers again because the yard work had needed doing and they'd been foot-loose and fancy free on Saturday a few weeks back.

Travis shook Cole's hand, and Jackie could see the approval shining in his eyes. "It's nice having you home."

"Thanks," Cole said, leaning his elbows on the table as the mayor walked away, meeting up with his wife, Donna, for a dance.

"I'll be leaving your reputation in good standing," Jackie said.

The silence between them grew, and she turned to watch Levi and Laura dance. She'd never felt awkward sitting in silence when she was with Cole, except lately. The countdown to her leaving Sweetheart Creek was looming, like a clock that grew louder with every tick. And her move had a date now, an address.

She'd have to tell him she'd found a place, but right now she wanted to enjoy these waning moments together, since each day felt more and more as though this thing between them was over.

Cole wasn't moving to the city and she wasn't staying here. There would be no point in asking him to come with her. He belonged here, and hadn't returned home after five years away just to turn around and leave again.

The song ended and Levi and Laura slipped into the empty chairs Jackie and Cole had saved for them.

"You're not dancing tonight?" Laura asked, out of breath.

"Maybe later," Jackie said.

"Hey, what do you think about selling off a few of those red Angus yearlings?" Levi asked Cole. "We could take the profit and pour it into purchasing a Beefmaster bull at the next auction." He was leaning on the table, ready to listen.

"Do we have enough to cover the increased feed costs for our lactating cows?"

Jackie rolled her eyes at Laura, gesturing to the brothers, even though her heart warmed at how they were fitting back into the old partnership they'd once had, being each other's best sounding board. She had a feeling the ranch was going to have some very good years ahead.

Just another reason not to follow her heart and ask him to leave with her.

"Ready to move to the city?" Laura asked gently.

Jackie sighed and scrunched up her nose. "Not especially." She gave a bright smile. "But Mrs. Fisher has been saving boxes from the diner's food orders so I can pack my things. I'm going to have the best-smelling belongings by the time I move."

She caught Cole watching her, his expression softening. He tapped her nose as she scrunched it again, trying to dispel the sadness that overcame her at the thought of moving away from all she had here.

"Careful, your face might freeze like that."

She laughed and wished he was sitting close enough that she could lean against his shoulder, spend every last second attached to him.

* * *

Laura and Levi went out for another spin around the dance floor as the crowd thinned out, the band finishing their last set for the night. Cole noticed his father sitting with a friend at the bar, every once in a while casting a glance his way.

"Do you think I should go talk to him?" Cole asked, just as Jackie started talking.

"I found an apartment," she blurted.

He set down his whiskey.

He'd convinced himself this moment wouldn't actually come. That she wouldn't really pack up her belongings and Goose, and try to fit into city life.

Daisy-Mae strode past in the same outfit she'd worn on New Year's Eve, looking very much the buckle bunny. She stopped, backtracked and asked over her shoulder, "You two need anything? Last call in fifteen."

They shook their heads and she carried on.

"I have a week of overlap between my move and my dad's, so I can get set up," Jackie said. Her eyes were unfocused, the words coming out almost as though she was reading them from a script.

"You're really going to do this?" he asked, unable to look up from his whiskey. He wanted to stand up and shout at her, drag her home and make love to her all night. He wanted to rage, to tell her she couldn't possibly go, that she shouldn't leave him. Didn't she understand that what they had was special? How could she just give it up?

She gave him an angry look. "He's my father."

Cole exhaled harshly. He understood sacrificing for family. It just didn't seem fair that his life was being derailed once again by such a sacrifice.

"Did you find a job?"

Her shoulders slumped and she fidgeted with her glass.

"I'm sure you'll find one."

"I applied for a few online, but haven't heard back. Nobody wants a feed store lackey in the city."

"Will you come back when..." Cole pushed back from the table, letting out a long breath. He didn't want to finish the sentence, to plan for when her father was no longer in her life. That was callous, selfish and possibly the worst thing he could say.

Jackie had pushed back her chair as well, and now she stood.

"Jackie, don't." He felt desperate to stretch out every moment he had with her from now until she left.

She looked conflicted, and he realized he didn't know if he was asking her to not leave the saloon or the town. But mostly it was him. He didn't want her to leave him.

This was a breakup, and he'd never felt like this before when a relationship ended. Never. Not once. Not even an inkling of this.

"I'm sorry I couldn't do the long-term thing for you. I'm sure everything will work out fine for you from here on out."

Except he'd be doing it all without her at his side.

He stood, unsure what else to do. She rested a hand gently against his chest and leaned in to kiss him. The contact was brief, warm, and a goodbye.

Her lips quivered as though holding in a flood of emotion. "Me leaving is probably for the best." She gestured futilely. "There will be no gossip, no big ending and no..."

No being a wonderful boyfriend and doing what felt right. Following her. Staying with her.

But he wasn't cut out for the city. He'd tried that. He'd try again for Jackie, but she hadn't asked. Although, even if she had, he was fairly certain putting two miserable-to-be-there country folks in a city apartment would be a surefire way to end things, like someone throwing gasoline on a bonfire.

But Jackie? She'd make the best of it, bring a ray of sunshine everywhere she went and make San Antonio better for having her in it.

"We could do long-distance," she suggested lightly, such sadness etching her face that her laugh lines looked like ones of sorrow. Her eyes kept cutting to Laura and Levi, who were locked together in a slow dance, arms tight around each other like they were afraid to let go. They made it work because the two of them could flex their schedules and follow each other wherever the other needed to be. If Levi was needed on the ranch, Laura changed her New York meetings to ones online, keeping the internet humming with the quick exchange of contracts and other documents. If Laura was needed for an in-person meeting in New York or across the globe, Levi handed the reins to Myles and off he went.

Cole and Jackie couldn't do that.

But most of all, she meant too much to him to run her through the wringer.

"I told you in the beginning I'm not made for commitments," he joked, his light tone causing a sharp ache in his chest. He waited for her to look back at him, watching her from under the brim of his hat. "Let's not hurt each other by trying to make this work." She opened her mouth to argue, a flash in her eyes. "It's time for us to move on."

Patches of red appeared on her cheeks.

"Jackie, I'm trying not to hurt you." He felt desperate, like he was making the wrong choice, saying the wrong things. He was trying so hard to be a good man, to not let his old self rear up and fight.

And why did this hurt so much? They'd known this moment was coming.

"And this…" She gestured to him and the surrounding saloon, which was filled with friends and neighbors. Quite a few who were acting as though they weren't eavesdropping. "This doesn't hurt?"

This was where he had to be strong. This was where he had to put her needs before his.

She was waiting for him to speak, to find a way to make this work. He couldn't think of a darn thing. It was like standing at the edge of the flooding creek watching Ryan vanish under the muddy waters. Watching the horror unfold, unable to stop it.

"You don't follow someone to the city after dating for two and a half months," he said gently. "And long distance won't work. Not for us." Especially judging from how they'd started shutting down their hearts over the past month instead of growing closer, clinging to what they had. There wasn't anything for either of them to fight for, and they both knew it.

"The fantasy is over, Jackie." He swallowed hard, reached down and took a gulp of his whiskey, hoping the burn of it would become more prominent than the persistent ache in his chest. "It's been fun, but it's time."

Jackie's chin went up in defiance, as though she was impenetrable, as though he couldn't hurt her. But he knew better. It was an act.

He had hurt her. He'd hurt her by trying to protect her.

* * *

Jackie couldn't believe Cole had given up on them so easily. She knew he felt the same way she did, and yet he was being so stubborn about not even trying to find a solution, a way to make things work.

She leaned against the outer wall of the saloon, swiping at the tears running down her face. Rusty sat at her feet with a whine. She ignored him, heading home. In her apartment she began heaving clothing into boxes. She still had almost two weeks before she moved, but she needed to stay busy, to distract herself from the ease of Cole's rejection.

She'd wanted him to say he wasn't ever going to leave her corner, that he'd always be there, ready to fight, ready to protect, ready to solve.

She tried to cajole herself into believing a smooth breakup now was for the best, but couldn't help but wonder what might've happened if she'd found a way to stay in Sweetheart Creek.

11

Cole placed the last box of Jackie's things on the floor in her cluttered apartment. It was smaller than her one above the store in Sweetheart Creek, and felt cramped. He'd been driving one of the first trucks to arrive in the caravan of friends, and had helped roll out her area rugs, haul up her couch, armchair and bed, before bringing up boxes from other vehicles.

Goose sat on Jackie's purse, watching it all with a morose expression, his tail thumping whenever Cole walked past.

In the small kitchen, Mrs. Fisher and Cole's mom had already unpacked Jackie's dishes, stacking them on the counter as they debated the most logical and efficient place to store each item.

Mrs. Fisher flicked a light switch. When nothing happened, she flicked it a few more times, then moved to the fridge and checked the interior. She frowned and called Jackie. "Why don't you have electricity, honey?"

"I don't?"

"Did you get it hooked up?" Cole asked.

"What do you mean?" She looked so confused it broke his heart.

"It doesn't always come with your apartment." He'd learned that the hard way, too.

"I didn't have to hook it up in Sweetheart Creek," Jackie said, clearly miffed by this embarrassing oversight.

"Welcome to the city, sweetie. You pay for everything here. Even parking." Laura had hung up Jackie's clothes in the mirrored bedroom closet and now gave her a sympathetic smile.

"I can help you get it sorted out," Carly offered, popping up from the floor, where she'd finished putting the legs back on Jackie's coffee table.

"Well, go now," Maria said. "This food won't last forever without a refrigerator."

The two friends hustled out the door, purses slung over their shoulders, while the rest of the gang stayed behind, Levi attaching her bookshelf to the wall so that Brant and April could fill it up.

It was going to take Jackie days to find everything even though the apartment was small. Too small. And not nearly sunny enough. Plus the hallway to her apartment door smelled funny, and Cole didn't like the way her neighbor two doors down had eyed Jackie as if she was next on his dating list.

Cole had growled at the man, who'd stepped back into his apartment, locking the door. Too bad Cole wouldn't be here on a regular basis to remind the guy to stay in his little hole and away from his girlfriend.

Although he supposed he couldn't call her that any longer, and it was officially none of his business who she dated.

The realization gutted him, and he had to take a moment to collect himself.

By the time Jackie and Carly returned, the last box had been flattened and set out for recycling, and the women had put away the kitchenware, as well as cleaned up after the lunch they'd brought along for the helpers.

Now everyone was hugging Jackie and making their way to the door.

Too fast. It had all been too fast.

There were no more excuses to be with Jackie, to keep her in his arms, to suck out the last of being together.

With a sympathetic frown, Jenny Oliver closed the apartment door behind her, and Cole turned to Jackie. She was standing near the doorway to her minuscule kitchen, hands shoved deep in her jeans pockets. She looked exhausted and glum. They'd barely seen each other since The Goodbye, as he thought of their whiskey night in The Watering Hole, the past two weeks feeling like the longest of his life.

"Your dad moves next week?" he asked, not knowing what else to say to the woman he'd always found so easy to talk to.

She nodded.

"I heard they haven't found anyone for your job at the feed store yet. Are you going to commute until you find something here?" He was unable to disguise the hope in his voice.

"I got an entry position at a library a few blocks from here. Karen wrote me a glowing reference. The pay sucks, but it'll keep my head above water until I find something else."

Jackie looked up at the ceiling, blinking as her eyes filled with tears, her chin quivering. Cole had her in his arms in a second, holding her close. He stroked her hair, wanting to kiss her strawberry-scented lips. "It'll all work out. It'll be okay."

"You can't promise that," she said, shuddering.

"I know, but it will. Only good things happen to Jackie Moorhouse."

She gave a watery laugh. "I think the universe must have me confused with someone else then."

He tipped her chin up and dropped the sweetest of kisses on her lips. "The universe has never known what to do with you because you're able to blast your way through any wall." He stroked her cheek with a thumb, knowing that living in San Antonio was the only way for Jackie, or else she would have moved a mountain to have it differently. Just like he would have. "Keep smiling, sweetheart."

A sob broke from her, and it was like a spear driven into Cole's chest. He'd failed her. As emotion tore him apart, he vowed that he would make this better. He didn't know how, only that this time he was going to fight.

* * *

Exhausted, Jackie fell onto her couch, dropping her purse on the floor. Her dad was moving to the city in four days. She had gone to the new memory-care facility after her second day at the library, to finalize paperwork and take a box of his belongings ahead of time to help him transition. One of the facility's residents had been having a bad day, and an hour later, his screams were still echoing through her heart.

Jackie rolled onto her side and fished her phone from her purse. Her lock screen showed a picture of her and Cole cheek to cheek, grinning into the camera. She missed him. She missed everything about him, from the way he made her laugh, to feeling safe and secure, to being loved and cared for.

She turned onto her back again, setting her phone on her stomach. The ceiling above her was marked and stained. In the distance she heard sirens, and someone shuffling down the hallway. The sounds of the city were different, foreign, making her feel more alone.

Goose, who had barely left her bedroom since the move, came padding in, jumped up on the end of the couch and curled up on her feet.

Last night, Daisy-Mae, Jenny, Karen and Carly had made a foray into the city, scooping her up and taking her out for Tex-Mex near the Alamo. It was as though they'd known she'd need the soothing effect of friends after her first day in a new job, miles from everything familiar.

Not that she'd admit it to Karen, but the library work was mind-numbingly boring. Nobody was chatty, and there had been no interruptions like at the feed store in Sweetheart Creek, where someone she knew was always filtering through with a hello and some news. In the library, she'd spent the entire day taking stacks of books from the reshelving cart and placing them back where they belonged.

But it was an income. Money that would keep her close to her father.

As homesickness threatened to overwhelm her, she sat up and started making a mental list of ways she could make the city feel like it was her home. Instead of returning to Sweetheart Creek on the weekend like she'd planned, she was going to stay in her new neighborhood. She was going to introduce herself to at least one of her neighbors, even if she had to set up a chair in the hallway and wait for someone to come by. She was going to have coffee in the coffee shop down the block and learn the name of one barista, and fill in ten new job applications.

Take the city by the horns, show the universe she was going to blast through walls, like Cole believed she could.

She lifted her phone again as she lay back on the couch, her eyes watering as she took in her lock screen photo once again. Squeezing her phone, Jackie closed her eyes and made a secret wish, hoping that what Cole said about her and the universe was true. And that someday, somehow, she'd find her way back to the man she loved.

* * *

"You're okay with Jackie moving to the city?"

Cole looked up from where he was holding a calf against the Texas soil so Brant could quickly check its tag. His brother nodded and Cole released the animal, which skittered and bolted back to the herd. The brothers were a fast team, a necessity to keep them safe in case a calf's mother charged.

"I forgot I was her keeper," Cole retorted. "Maybe I should ask if *you're* okay with Jackie leaving."

He was well aware that he was once again "single," and that fact might make his brother nervous if he listened to the local gossip. All it had taken was for Cole to sit with April and Kurt for a minute or two in the diner yesterday, while waiting for Brant. Voilà! Rumors and speculation had started.

"I'm fine," Brant said, an edge to his voice.

"You know I'm not interested in April."

His brother chuckled, his spine relaxing again. "I know."

"What's that tone supposed to mean?" He'd seen the look on Brant's face when Cole had walked through the ranch house door on Christmas Day. His brother hadn't been happy to see him. Usually the most warm and welcoming one in the family, Brant was still a tad aloof with him. Plus he hadn't matched Cole with a dog yet, which was telling.

"Nothing." Brant closed his medical bag and strapped it to his saddle. Wordlessly the brothers mounted their horses and began the ride back to the ranch.

The silence ate at Cole. "Jackie moving wasn't my decision."

"The two of you looked like you were in it for the long haul."

It had felt like it, too. They hadn't ever fought, like he had with April. With her it had always felt like he was on quicksand, and one false move would get him sucked in. Being with Jackie had been so easy it had been almost surreal. Was it because they'd built their relationship on a fake foundation?

He didn't think so. They'd started off fake, but everything from that first kiss onward had been real for him. They'd told themselves it was pretend so they could protect themselves from their fears.

Yet he had hurt her, just as he'd predicted. But instead of a fight hurting her, he'd done the opposite and not fought. Which made no sense. He'd been so careful with her, striving to not repeat his past mistakes. And he'd still blown it.

He could have gone the distance with Jackie. And now she was in San Antonio and he was here.

"You're not going to do something long-distance?" Brant asked.

"It wasn't real. Not like that." He waited for his brother to argue, holding his breath, hoping. "Easy come, easy go."

The words felt like a lie, heavy in his chest.

"It was real, and it scares you." They were heading up a short embankment and Brant's horse leaped ahead, taking the slope in bounds. At the top, Brant turned and waited. Cole's horse had aged in the years he'd been away, and was now slower, more careful.

"You love her?" Brant said, making it a question. "And you're letting her go, why?"

Cole rubbed his face and scratched his ear. "Let's not do this, okay?" He guided his horse along the top of the embankment and toward the gate that would lead them to the farmyard.

"You and April sure did a number on each other," Brant said. The horses ambled side by side, tired from chasing the herd all morning. Cole longed to break into a gallop and leave his brother behind. "But she's found happiness, and she's healing. I thought you were, too."

"Brant," Cole warned. He really didn't need his brother prying into his emotions right now. Or ever.

"I thought you and Jackie had found love."

"She needs to be in the city with her dad."

They rode silently for a moment longer, the hooves of their horses quiet on the damp earth. Around them the countryside had come to life, green, fresh and bright, promising a new season of hope for the ranch and its prosperity.

"You were asked for space, and you gave everyone way too much," Brant finally said, speaking of the past.

Cole sighed and gritted his teeth, tamping down emotion. "If I recall, you thought I shouldn't."

"You're right, and I'm sorry about that," he said cheerfully. "I thought you should stay with April, and I'm thankful every day that you didn't listen to me." He grinned, and Cole couldn't help but release some of his own tension as a result. His brother was happy. Good coming from the bad. Life was working out for two people he loved. That should be enough.

Even if the powers that be didn't seem to think it was his time to find the same.

"But with Jackie…" Brant grew quiet.

"What about her?" Cole asked at long last, knowing he was taking the bait by asking his brother for more of his thoughts on the matter of his ill-fated romance.

"I don't think she needs or wants space. The opposite, maybe."

"I have responsibilities here."

"Family is important," Brant agreed quietly, his blue eyes searching Cole's for answers.

Cole's time away from April had allowed her to become her true self. A woman who was stable and strong. He wondered what Jackie would become now that she had some time away from him. Would she change, too?

"She belongs in Sweetheart Creek," Brant stated.

"I know." Cole glowered at him.

"So bring her home. Or at the very least don't lose out on everything because you think we can't get along here without you."

"You want me to leave?" Cole asked, watching his brother for a tell.

Brant looked as though he was dealing with an imbecile. "You don't get it, do you?" he said at long last.

"I can't take over her life." April had always ridden him about doing that in their relationship. It had caused most of their fights.

"Now you decide to change?" Brant let out a frustrated growl and shook his head.

"April used to yell at me over this stuff."

They had stopped at the gate, but instead of dismounting, Brant leaned forward, hands stacked on the saddle horn. "This is the one time you're supposed to take charge and be that bossy so-and-so we all love to hate."

Cole's horse sidestepped at Brant's gruff tone and Cole reined him back in, considering the suggestion. Brant was the brother most in tune with his feelings and those of others.

Did he really think Cole should boss Jackie around and solve her problems? Assuming there was a solution, of course.

It made no sense, though. She hadn't asked him to stay with her.

In fact, she hadn't asked him for anything.

Hadn't asked anyone for anything.

Why was that?

"So I'm supposed to waltz in and tell her what to do with her life? That sounds like a good way to get a cowboy boot implanted up my butt."

Brant laughed, swinging down from the saddle to open the gate. "Go solve her problems, Cole. Jackie needs it." Their gazes met as Cole led Brant's horse through the gate alongside his own. "Jackie needs you."

The words echoed through his mind for the rest of the ride back to the stable.

* * *

"Hon, maybe it's time to give up on him." Mrs. Fisher looked worried, her eyebrows pinched together.

Jackie lifted her elbows off the diner's back counter and

straightened her spine, trying to pull herself together. It just felt like so much effort to remain upbeat. She'd been in the city for a few days now and had given up on her Sunday task list of applying for jobs. Instead, she'd climbed into her car and driven out to Riverbend to visit her dad, whose moving date had been switched to Thursday. He'd slept the entire time she was there.

Feeling down, Jackie had continued on to Sweetheart Creek in hopes that her old hometown would boost her spirits. She hadn't told Cole she was coming. She hadn't told anyone.

"It's not about Cole," she said to Mrs. Fisher. But it was. She missed him. Even more than this town, than her old job. She gave a lighthearted wave. "That was just… fun."

"Your dad moves tomorrow?" Mrs. Fisher asked.

She shook her head. "They pushed the date back a few days."

"You look down," Laura said, sliding onto the stool beside her. "I like your outfit." She took in Jackie's pajama pants and T-shirt, her messy ponytail. "Um, your boots, I mean."

"I feel like I got run over, then dragged through the mud," Jackie admitted.

"But it's not about Cole," Mrs. Fisher stated, her tone saying she disagreed.

"Then it's probably just the effect of learning that such a long-standing crush wasn't real?" Laura's voice lifted in question. Jackie caught her giving Mrs. Fisher a worried glance. "You know, like, uh… disappointment? Like when you meet a hot actor in real life and it turns out he's actually short."

"It was just a crush," Jackie confirmed, then tried to swallow the lump in her throat. "I'm over it."

"You were chasing the idea of that man for a lot of years, Jackie. It was bound to happen." Mrs. Fisher's lips pulled into a thin line. "Best to mosey on down the line to the next one, dear. Put Cole Wylder in your rearview mirror."

Laura's eyes filled with sympathy as she watched Jackie struggle for a cheery smile.

"Yup," Jackie said. "That's what I'll do."

"It was never real, and you're a smart gal." Mrs. Fisher's tone was firm, leaving no room for argument. "Put the fantasy aside now that you've seen the truth."

The problem was that she *had* seen the truth. Cole was special. He was the man she loved.

"It was fun, now it's over." Mrs. Fisher slapped her dish towel on the counter in front of Jackie and she jumped. "You've wasted too much time brooding over a man who probably would have run away in the end, anyway. Where's the Jackie we know?"

She nodded, unable to speak.

Laura's warm hand covered her own. "I know moving away is hard. If you need anything let me know, okay? We're all still here for you. We don't mind zipping down the highway to join you for a cup of coffee, or help you hang some pictures on your walls." She lowered her voice. "Or eat chunky fudge ice cream."

Jackie nodded, swallowing her heartbreak. She stood and exited the diner, then stared down the street, realizing she had nowhere to go. No job. No home just a few blocks away, as it had already been rented out. No boyfriend. Just an apartment an hour and a half away.

She saw the faded red Chevrolet from the Sweet Meadows Ranch round the corner by the hardware store and her heart hiccupped. She leaned forward, waiting to see who was driving. It was Maria. Jackie waved and continued toward her own car, stopping to stare at its bumper.

Maybe the thing with Cole truly had been just an infatuation or a crush, and she'd built it into something more in her head. Like the time in tenth grade when she'd thought she was going to go to college on a cheerleading scholarship, then didn't even make the regional team.

But if she'd just built it all up in her head, then it wouldn't hurt like this, right? She should feel as though she'd been set free by the knowledge that it had been only a crush.

Instead, all she felt was hurt.

She straightened her shoulders. Even if it had ended quickly, Cole had been worth it. He'd been even better than her fantasies, and now that she knew what love felt like she could go find it in San Antonio.

12

Cole tightened the wire on the small pen near the back stables where they kept ailing calves or lambs as needed. Discovering the ranch now had sheep had been a surprise, especially since Levi seemed to have such a love-hate relationship with them. In fact, his brother had insisted they fix this pen in case his little wooly friends needed it.

Levi had found a lot of things to keep Cole busy now that all was forgiven, and the workload around the ranch had definitely increased. So far it hadn't worked as an effective distraction from missing Jackie, though. She'd been gone a week, and it felt like a year, each day harder than the last.

His talk with Brant had made Cole feel as though he should do something about Jackie—for Jackie. But his well of ideas had run dry before he'd even finished brushing down his horse after the ride.

He'd heard she'd been in town yesterday, looking miserable and a shell of her former self.

Being away from him and the town wasn't good for her. She wasn't thriving. Wasn't growing stronger or finding herself, like April had when he'd left.

Jackie needed to be here. But it seemed Fate had decided she was supposed to be in San Antonio without him.

Alone.

Again.

There had to be a solution. Maybe he should just pack a bag, show up on her doorstep and refuse to leave.

He sighed, hating how everything on this ranch reminded him of Jackie, even from their teenage days. Like the time she'd dared him to jump off the roof of this stable into the back of a truck loaded with hay. He'd refused, and she'd teased him unrelentingly for the rest of the day. Come to think of it, he hadn't minded the attention from her. She'd always been fun, and gorgeous. The problem was he now knew she was so much more than that.

"Ouch!" Levi yelped, and Cole looked over. At some point he'd let go of the wire he was stretching, and it had spooled itself back toward his brother, slapping him in the face.

Cole swore under his breath, worried the wire's sharp edge could have taken out his brother's eye. "You all right? I forgot you were here."

"Where's your head? You've been out of it for days and it's becoming dangerous." Levi's face was red, and he stepped back, dropping his tools on the ground.

"Sorry." He took the wire and began stretching it again, embarrassed for tuning out so thoroughly.

"Seriously. What's your deal?"

"No deal," Cole said, not looking at him.

"I'm going to die an early death if I keep you on this ranch."

Cole finally looked over, judging the level of threat.

Levi sighed, then said, "Well?"

"I'm sorry. Maybe I should go inside and take a break."

"No."

Cole winced, certain this was it. Kicked out.

He felt the beginning of a smile. If Levi asked him to leave the ranch he could move to San Antonio, guilt free.

And then what?

Be miserable alongside Jackie? He'd overheard Laura telling Levi in the kitchen that she was unhappy and had looked glum. But what had stung even more was that Jackie hadn't told Cole she was coming to town. He'd thought they'd at least stay friends.

Maybe he shouldn't show up on her doorstep.

Cole realized Levi was talking to him. "What?"

"You've got it bad, don't you?" His brother shook his head, pushed his hat back and rubbed his forehead. "Laura was right." He let out a small sound of disbelief, then grinned. "Who would have thought?"

Cole didn't speak, just watched him, waiting for clues.

"You love her."

"No! Laura's *your* girl."

"I meant Jackie," Levi said patiently. "I've never seen you like this. Not even with April." He was shaking his head again. "Boy, I sure was wrong, wasn't I?"

Cole frowned, hoping he would explain.

Levi didn't.

"Yup, Jackie's the gal for you." He picked up the tools and began walking away.

"We're not finishing the pen?" One side was still slack, pushed down by gravity, age, tall grass and likely a large sheep or two.

"Later. You've got a woman to win back."

"There's no winning back," Cole said, his chest aching as he looked up into the blue sky above.

"Why not?"

"We didn't end like that. She needs to be in the city and I need... to be here," he said softly.

"You really are stupid."

"Excuse me?" Cole was instantly on the defensive, ready to fight. He and Levi had gotten into scuffles as teens, and he wouldn't mind one now. Anything would be a welcome distraction from the pain in his heart.

"She doesn't belong there."

"I didn't say she did," Cole retorted. This was like talking to Brant all over again.

"You need to go get her."

"She needs to be with her dad."

"Speaking of dads, ours seems to be looking for you."

Cole stilled, scanning the yard for their father. Levi pointed toward the stable. Roy was shifting from foot to foot, hands deep in his pockets.

"See what he wants, then come find me. I think I might know about something you don't." He grinned. "Or else it'll just prove to me you're even dumber than I thought."

"Levi…" Cole warned, hands on his hips. He really didn't have patience for any teasing right now. If Levi had a way for him to be with the woman who had captured his heart, he wanted to hear it immediately.

* * *

Instead of pummeling his brother for information, Cole forced himself to walk over to their dad, willing himself to be patient.

At the moment it didn't matter that Jackie hadn't asked him to join her in San Antonio. She hadn't asked anything of anyone.

He could see his mistakes more clearly now. He should have pushed himself upon her, told her he loved her. He should have stopped trying to be the man he thought everyone wanted him to be, and done what had felt right in his heart. He should have made demands, and acted like the man Jackie had been chasing since elementary school.

As Cole approached, he saw how age had crept up on Roy Wylder over the past five years. Small changes, from the slight stoop of his once square shoulders, to the hesitancy as he braced for what could be a nasty confrontation.

Cole didn't have anger left for this. It had burned out a long time ago. So, for his father's sake, maybe it was time to mend this fence. Or just knock it down and burn the remains, since being ignored by his dad since Christmas hadn't felt awesome.

Okay, so there might be a tad bit of anger left.

"I was hoping to catch you," Roy said stiffly. "There are some things I'd like to discuss."

"Dad," Cole warned. His father had made himself very clear about how Cole had let him down by not protecting April all those years ago. Roy, an old cowboy, had believed Cole should have done a better job of protecting her, his woman, a member of the Wylder family. But Cole's father had let *him* down during what had been a mounting crisis, and that was so much worse.

"No," he said sternly. "I know I said some awful things. I sent you away from this town, your family. Trust me that the women in my life have made it abundantly clear how I was in the wrong. The only thing keeping me from making it right has been my stupid cowboy pride."

"Mom?" Cole asked, knowing Maria hadn't been happy about the way the confrontation had gone down, or Cole's subsequent self-imposed exile. His parents had always displayed a united front, and it seemed weird that she might lay into Roy over her displeasure. "I didn't mean for things between me and April to come between you."

"I appreciate that, but a man makes his own mistakes. You don't get to take credit for mine."

That was kind of what April had been saying, too. And a lot of mistakes had been made that night five years ago.

"Sophia and April also had some thoughts on the matter." His father's tone suggested they'd definitely shared their opinions and not held back. The realization brought a slight smile to Cole's face. His father echoed it with a ghostly smile of his own before growing serious again. "I know now that what you did was for her, and that you made an enormous sacrifice. You're a good man, Cole. And it might sound odd given how I've behaved, but I am proud of you."

Roy's lips twisted and he inhaled sharply, as though trying to tuck his emotions back into place. "I'm sorry, son." He cleared his throat. "I should've come looking for you. Should've called. Probably should've listened, too, as you knew her best."

Cole tried to mask his amused expression. Listening wasn't one of his father's best traits.

"That's basically my life, though," Roy continued, his shoulders relaxing. "Seems like I tended to take the left path whenever I should've taken the right."

"I kind of like having been born, though," Cole said, letting the man off the hook ever so slightly by suggesting he hadn't completely messed up everything. Most things, but not quite all of it.

The corner of his father's mouth hinted at another smile. "It's good to have you home. I'm sorry you aren't staying longer so we can patch things up proper-like."

"What? I'm not leaving."

"You're not following Jackie?"

"No." How many times did he have to have this conversation?

Then again, maybe his family gave him more credit when it came to love than he deserved, and it was more about that than him mending fences.

"Oh. I thought that puppy from Brant was a going-away gift."

"Puppy?"

His father froze. "It was just talk."

Talk that suggested Cole had been accepted back into the family fold by the middle Wylder brother.

"You'll have to stop in for supper sometime if you're sticking around," his father said.

Cole nodded, even though his brain was suddenly screaming

"no" to staying on the ranch. He needed to be with Jackie. No matter what. Even if that meant leaving the acceptance he was finally finding. Because even though it was what he'd wanted for the past five years, it paled in comparison to having Jackie.

* * *

"You need to come with me. I have something to show you."

"What?" Jackie stood in her apartment doorway, staring at Cole.

He was here. In San Antonio. And he had something to show her.

No hello. No kiss. Just a command. So typical of the Cole Wylder she'd grown up with.

Man, she'd missed him.

But of course no kisses. They'd broken up.

She blinked at him, trying to register what was going on. He was as handsome as ever, but his expression was somber, and maybe even slightly nervous. Conflicting emotions threatened to overwhelm her.

He glanced past her, shifting from foot to foot, no doubt observing the embarrassing towers of takeout boxes littering her coffee table. She'd like to say she was making up for lost time, given the lack of takeout selections in Sweetheart Creek, but that would be a lie.

She was floundering. Despite checking her peephole whenever she heard a hallway noise, she had yet to meet any of her neighbors. Yes, she'd heard someone last Saturday and had popped out to say hi, but the woman had looked so frightened that Jackie had panicked and pretended she had to check her mailbox, then promptly locked herself out of her apartment.

"Um..." She tore her gaze away from Cole's delectable shoulders and looked at her wrist before realizing she wasn't wearing her step-counting watch. In fact, she was in her pajamas despite it being after nine on a Tuesday morning. She hugged her arms around herself and smoothed her tangled ponytail. She wasn't due at the library until her late-afternoon shift and had planned a full morning of wallowing.

She and Cole had rarely even texted since her move. What was he doing here?

"Trust me," he said, a hint of question in his voice.

She didn't want to. She needed to stay reined in, her barely bridled heart looking for its next escape. If she went anywhere with Cole it would bolt. And then she'd have a runaway heart once again, one she wasn't certain she could trick back into its pen a second time.

She needed to keep her feet rooted to the floor of this stupid, too-small apartment that overlooked a noisy street in a city that was at least ten degrees hotter than Hill Country at any given point in time.

Whatever she did, she needed to say no to Cole. Say no to hope.

Without realizing it, she'd slipped her hand into his extended one, his fingers closing around hers, warm and sure.

She could have sworn she saw a flicker of relief in his eyes.

She was still safe. Still inside her apartment. If she stepped outside of it, then she was going to get her hopes up, have them dashed, and then have even more reason to bury herself in chocolate ice cream. Laura had a lot of good ice cream recommendations and the local grocery store stocked them all. Chunky fudge, chocolate and raspberry swirl, chocolate chip cookie dough with caramel chips… The list was lengthy.

Jackie stepped over the threshold.

"Do you want to put some clothes on?" Cole asked, eyeing her with concern.

She nodded mutely. She could still close the apartment door, lock it, and ignore his pleading knocks.

On stiff legs, she headed to her bedroom and pulled on the

bibbed denim sundress she'd worn to work yesterday. She slipped into sandals, walked to her tiny bathroom and ran a damp cloth over her face and brushed out her ponytail. She told Goose to be good, and was out the door before she could allow any thoughts to roam through her numb mind.

Namely, the ones that would stop her from soaking up this gift of time with Cole.

She allowed him to lead her out into the blinding sunshine. Too bad Easter was long gone, as well as a big sale on chocolate, because she was fairly certain that after today's surprise she was going to need lots of it. And not just the frozen-milk-product kind.

Cole's truck was idling at the curb, no doubt to keep the cab nice and cool by running the air-conditioning. She laughed, thinking how you couldn't take the small town out of a man like Cole. He was willing to trust when he shouldn't.

He must have caught her look, as he said, "It's locked."

He proved it by punching the code into the door panel, unlocking the vehicle for them.

"Where are we going?"

"It's gonna take a few hours. Is that okay?" he asked, looking at her from the driver's seat. "Carly said you weren't working until this afternoon."

Now the strange text messages from Carly made sense. She'd been asking about her shifts and all sorts of other odd things.

Jackie's hopes buoyed, and she was eager to find out what had been planned between her friends. "Can you have me back by two?"

"Maybe."

She gave him a look.

"Well, I don't know. I've never done this before."

"And what are we doing?"

"Do you have your purse with you?"

"Why? Do I have to pay for gas?"

Cole's face relaxed, revealing just how worried and uncertain he'd been feeling. She patted her hip pocket, where her wallet still sat from yesterday. She'd bought herself coffee on the way to work. It had been odd, crossing the street, running a few doors down just like she did at home. But instead of the Longhorn Diner, where everyone knew her and a quick coffee could take a few hours if given the chance, she'd simply been a number in a long line of people not meeting each other's eyes.

"Where are we going?" she repeated as Cole pulled out into traffic.

"I'll show you."

Fifteen minutes later they were on the highway that led to Sweetheart Creek. Jackie stiffened in her seat. "I'm not moving back. I can't."

"I'm not asking you to."

That brought tears to her eyes, and she looked out the side window.

Cole, usually comfortable with silence, clicked on the radio. Willie Nelson filled the cab with his crooning about mamas not letting their babies to grow up to be cowboys. As they were always alone, even with others, and a person never knew how to take them. At the moment, the song felt fitting.

They turned before they reached Sweetheart Creek, heading deeper into Hill Country.

"Where are we going?" she asked once again, hoping for an answer this time.

"Somewhere I don't think you've been before."

"Murdered in a ravine?" She was rewarded with a smile.

Cole slowed not long after, taking a corner. Despite being officially in the middle of nowhere, he knew the route when she didn't, amplifying her curiosity as she lost track of where they were. Finally she recognized the Lone Oak Grill, a diner she and her father used to go to when she was a kid. It was closed now, its abandoned state saddening her. A minute later, Cole turned again where a herd of black cattle grazed in the shade of tall junipers.

In the distance, she could see a large circular building, with parked cars shining in the unrelenting Texas sun.

"I don't remember a big ranch being out here." It wasn't uncommon for the odd Texan family to have a giant, rambling ranch house worth more than the GDP of some third world countries. But she was certain that, this close to Sweetheart Creek, she would have heard about a home as enormous as the largest Malibu mansions.

"It's not a ranch."

When they neared the long winding drive he turned down it. Jackie closed her eyes, too much hope swelling inside her when she spotted the sign.

Cole stopped at a gate about twenty yards along. The entire estate didn't look institutional, despite its function. It was a memory-care facility in the middle of nowhere.

And only miles from Sweetheart Creek.

The man at the small outpost nodded at Cole and released the gates, allowing them to swing open so they could drive through.

"How did I not hear about this place?" It boasted neat landscaping that had yet to grow wild and out of control. The building's paint was fresh and bright, not yet beaten by the Texas rays.

"They opened eight months ago to test their new intensive, specialized facility, and to ensure a depth of training for all staff. They started with only a handful of patients who had been referred by their doctors. Two weeks ago they quietly opened up a few slots to new applicants. Eventually they will be fully open."

"But how did I not hear about it?" How did Dr. Gomez not know? Or anyone in Sweetheart Creek? Or had she been so close-lipped about her father's condition that nobody had thought to mention it to her, assuming she already knew and hadn't chosen it because surely a facility like this was beyond her budget?

"It was a closed system for months," Cole said simply. "Levi read an interview with the founder in one of those magazines they give you on airplanes. It was about his research on well-being and Alzheimer's, and Levi put two and two together after driving past this place the other day. So we came out here to see what the deal was. They're not even advertising yet."

Jackie turned in her seat, gazing out at an elderly man sitting on a bench, hand outstretched. Songbirds were flitting about, taking seeds from his palm as they dared.

"Can I afford it?" she whispered.

"It's less than what you'd pay in San Antonio, believe it or not."

She scanned the grounds again. The security. The natural setting. The apparent high staff-to-patient ratio of those sitting in a gazebo under some leafy trees near the side of the building. This seemed too good to be true.

"However, there might be a catch or two," Cole said.

There always was.

* * *

Jackie was in love with the facility. Cole could tell not just by the way she kept saying so, but by the way her shoulders had relaxed as they toured the grounds, that inner smile that made her glow returning. The staff believed in getting their residents outdoors as much as possible within the various enclosed natural spaces, sitting in the gardens, both indoor and outdoor, as well as keeping them active with simple games such as shuffleboard and bocce ball. There was lots of space, predictable routine to reduce stress, and numerous built-in safety elements that didn't feel institutional. The staff were smart, kind and well-trained. Various communal rooms were scented with essential oils such as lemon, bergamot and lavender instead of the usual stinging antiseptic smells.

And the best part was that as needs progressed, so did the staff's ability to meet them. It was also affordable and close. There was just one catch and Cole wasn't sure Jackie would like it.

"How do you keep the monthly fee so low?" Jackie asked, once they were settled inside the director's office. It was filled with plants and books, the large window behind the woman's maple desk letting in plenty of sunlight.

Jackie clutched the brochure she'd been given, her lips in a tight line. She was looking for the catch. The thing that would yank this dream away from her and her father.

"It's always cheaper to run something like this out in the boonies than in the city," the director said, her eyes shining with kindness. "Having a fair number of practicum students also helps, as I mentioned during our tour. We also have a number of trained volunteers who can work with residents who require less medical attention, particularly during meals and recreational time."

The director continued, "Of course, doctors and regular staff are always just around the corner. And for those with greater needs, our well-trained and experienced staff is readily available all hours of the day. We built this facility using donations and grants, so we aren't carrying debt. Our monthly staffing and groundskeeping costs are considerable, but with some creativity we've been able to make this a reality for the average county resident."

"Why aren't you full?"

"We're getting there," she said cautiously. "As Cole mentioned, we have just recently opened applications. As well, because of our bylaws, we can only accept Sweet Hills County residents."

"My dad's lived here all his life," Jackie said, leaning forward in her chair.

"Those restrictions also extend to family members. We are a

facility that values family input and therefore require that at least one of your father's next of kin lives in the county. This facility was sponsored by an area family who wanted to provide something for locals." She was looking straight at Jackie and Cole held his breath, knowing this was the catch, the part that could break her. "They know how many families have to uproot from the community they've always lived in in order to receive proper care for their loved one. There is absolutely no flexibility on this policy."

"Both Jackie and her father have lived in Sweet Hills County all their lives," Cole said.

"No problem then." The director smiled.

"Where do I sign?" Jackie asked, feeling slightly desperate, as though this dream situation might be ripped from her.

"The application process is quite involved, but we can hold your father's spot while we do that. All we need is your proof of residency."

Jackie tensed.

"That shouldn't be a problem," Cole said. "Do you want a legal land description, or something with our mailing address from a tax notice or something?"

"I don't have those," Jackie whispered. She'd frozen, and Cole sent her a silent message to remain quiet. He had this.

"Jackie's always been a Sweetheart Creek townie, but she just moved out onto the family ranch with me," Cole said, locking his hand around hers. He gave it a squeeze, and she squeezed back so tightly she almost cut off the circulation in his fingers. "As my girlfriend, her name isn't on any of the ranch's paperwork, but we are county residents." Cole turned to Jackie, who had gone pale. "Maybe Terry can vouch that you rented his place above the store for the past six years?"

"That should suffice," the director said, eyeing them. "Your landlord's letter to establish long-standing residency, and your new legal land description and mailing address to verify your current one along with your father's records from the Riverbend facility."

Jackie's grip on Cole's hand was so strong it was like being squeezed by a bull in a chute. He wrapped his free hand over hers, wordlessly letting her know that everything would be okay, that he'd fixed this for her because he loved her.

* * *

Jackie couldn't believe it. Stunned, she walked to the front doors of the facility. She could hear herself chatting, being amicable, but inside she was freaking out.

She had moved onto the ranch with Cole?

That was a lie!

They weren't even dating at the moment.

She had moved to the city. Miles and miles away. Counties away!

Her father wasn't eligible to live in this amazing building with this incredible staff and all this nature. He was moving in two days to San Antonio, where she was going to spend a third more money for not-as-good care.

She wanted him in this facility, desperately. Gerry Lee would be living peacefully, and his old friends could still visit him easily. He'd be in nature, something that had always soothed him.

In the parking area, she turned to look at the sprawling building once again, pinching her arm.

It couldn't be real.

It wasn't real.

She didn't live in Sweet Hills County any longer.

The only way to get her father into this place was to lie like Cole had.

He was watching her from his side of the truck and she stared at him for a long moment.

Wordlessly, they both climbed in and drove down the fresh

asphalt once again, nodding to the gatekeeper before turning out onto the gravel road.

Jackie's thoughts swirled. She could move back into the county, work in any old dead-end job to support her father living here. His savings might even cover most of the cost.

But Cole... What was he offering? How much of what he'd told the director was real? How much was a lie?

Two miles down, at the abandoned diner, she said, "Stop the truck."

She needed air.

As soon as Cole braked she was out and on the move, the heat from the cracked asphalt parking lot under her sandaled feet warming her legs, her torso. A light breeze ruffled her hair as she turned to him.

Cole was standing near the truck door, hands in his pockets.

"What was all of that?" she asked.

He licked his lips and slowly made his way over to where she had stopped, beside a faded sign for homemade pie.

"The truth."

"The truth?" She felt wild inside. The lies. The secrets. The conflicting hope and desire to make that facility her father's new home. The hint that Cole loved her with the depth in which she loved him. It was all too much.

"Maybe not today's truth, but I'm hoping it'll be tomorrow's?" He tilted his head to the side, as if curious about how she'd react.

She felt blindsided. Like a bus had hit her.

"Tomorrow's?" she said weakly, exhausted from holding back her hope, and no longer able to process what he was hinting at.

"Jackie." Cole licked his lips again, his chest expanding as he said, "I want this for you, for your dad."

"So do I, but I can't lie. I can't pretend to live on the ranch when I live in the city." She muttered to herself, "I'll move back, obviously. Use your address for the time being, and hope they don't discover the truth. Or tell them the truth… I could do that.

Just admit I was going to move because there was nowhere for my dad to stay in the county, and that I moved right back again when this spot opened up. I'll tell them we broke up. That's not a lie. A deposit could hold my dad's spot while I work out the application details."

"Or you could just use my address," Cole said, when she finally finished rambling.

Her head snapped up so quickly she nearly saw spots dancing in her vision. "What?" she whispered.

He tentatively placed his hands on her hips. "Move in with me."

"So my dad can live there?" She pointed down the road.

"And so you can live with me."

Jackie sucked in a lungful of air. She couldn't focus, couldn't think what his words might mean. What they didn't mean.

She should have stayed in her apartment. Should have soldiered on with that awful city life and facility. A sob of despair bubbled in her chest, tight and painful.

Cole tenderly cupped her chin, tipping her face upward so she'd look at him. "I love you, Jackie."

"Wha-what?" She swallowed hard, blinking. Her voice was hoarse, as if she'd been hiking through the desert for days without water.

"I love you." He was smiling, amusement dancing in his eyes.

Yes, she thought she'd heard that part correctly.

"You do?"

"I do. Will you move in with me?"

"That's really… That's fast. Sudden. I mean, we broke up. This whole fake thing… we really need to end that because I'm getting very confused." She broke from his loose grip, her brain refusing to catch up with what Cole might be saying, meaning.

"I stopped pretending a long time ago, Jackie. I'm not sure when exactly, but I think it might have been the day we fixed your bumper."

"Valentine's Day? You fell in love with me on Valentine's Day?"

"Don't look so frantic." He chuckled, but she could see he was freaking out inside at the way she was having issues getting a grip on herself.

"You're sure?"

"Jackie." Cole snagged her hand and drew her close, his proximity settling her. "I love you. I want to help you and make you happy. I want to solve your problems and cause you new ones."

"What? Why?"

"Just making sure you're listening."

She smacked his chest, feeling her concerns and worries ebb like the sea at low tide.

"Jackie, will you be my not-fake girlfriend?"

She felt the weight of the world lift from her shoulders, realizing that in this moment she might actually have it all. Everything she wanted. And more.

It was even sweeter than she'd dreamed it would be.

"I'd like to keep you for longer than the end of May. Would that be okay with you?"

Jackie inhaled, allowing all her hope and happiness to unfold and put her back together again. And love. Lots of love.

"Cole, it would be my pleasure to help keep you happily committed to one woman for a very long time. Like, so long it'll scare the both of us."

"How about forever?" he asked, scooping her up in a hug that lifted her feet off the ground.

She laughed, her heart feeling free. "That sounds like a good start. When shall I move in?"

"Tomorrow. Tonight."

"So soon?"

"Jackie," Cole said, suddenly serious. He set her down on her feet again. "I don't want to spend another minute without you."

"Oh."

He dropped to one knee. "I don't have a ring yet, but will you marry me?"

She laughed, covering her mouth, knowing she was gaping.

Cole.

Cole had asked her to marry him.

Cole Wylder.

For real. Not for pretend. For no other reason than he loved her.

"Jackie?"

She blinked, unable to overcome the shock.

"Did I break you?" he asked.

She nodded, and he laughed.

"So, JackieLynn? Will you marry me?"

"I don't think moving this fast will help your reputation, you know. Have you thought this through?"

His expression fell.

"I'm kidding! Yes! Yes, I'll marry you, Cole!"

He let out a breath of relief.

"Maybe before I move in, we should talk to your family."

"I already did."

"You did?"

He nodded. "I told them my plan."

"Even this part?"

"No. This part was spontaneous." He held up her bare ring finger. "I'll have to fix this."

"Nothing too big, okay?"

"Okay."

"And so what did your family say about your plan?"

"They asked me what I was waiting for, and all but filled my truck with gas and handed me the keys so I'd get to the city and sweep you up."

Jackie laughed. "You lie."

"Not about this." And then he gave her a kiss that told her

everything she needed to know about just how serious he was when it came to how much he loved her.

* * *

Cole dropped his fiancée off in San Antonio with what was likely a world-record-breaking long kiss goodbye, and a promise to return in the morning with boxes to help her move home after she worked tonight's shift at the library before letting them know she was quitting. As he drove back through the beautiful Texas Hill Country he felt as though everything was falling into place for the first time since he'd come home to Sweetheart Creek.

When he'd started the fake relationship with Jackie, he'd had no idea it would turn out like this. That he would find what he was looking for. Something he hadn't even known he needed.

As he turned down the driveway to Sweet Meadows Ranch, he marveled at the fact that tomorrow this would be Jackie's home. His and Jackie's. It felt right. Fast, just the way he liked things, and so very right.

He was getting married.

He let out a laugh and added his truck to the row of pickups lined up near the ranch house porch, between Brant's and one he recognized as his father's.

His mood faltered slightly. He'd been mending fences, but didn't particularly want to see Roy on the happiest day he'd had in a very long time.

Cole got out of his truck, his boots crunching the gravel underfoot. A shadow on the porch moved forward into the sunlight and down the steps. Cole worked to calm his breathing and slowly closed his truck door. His father stopped a few feet away.

"How did it go?" Roy asked.

Cole stared at him. "Sorry?"

"Brant said you went to help Jackie. I was sad to hear about her dad's condition, and how she had to move to the city. That's tough on a country girl."

He nodded.

"I heard you changed things for her today?"

"She's moving home."

"Good." The corner of Roy's's mouth turned up in a smile. "And I hear she was... happy with your meddling?"

Ah, the Sweetheart Creek rumor mill. Would there be anyone left for him to tell about his engagement?

"She was."

His father stepped closer, his cowboy boots disturbing the dirt at his feet. For a moment, Cole thought he was going to hug him.

Roy cleared his throat and held up his hand, fingers closed, palm down. "This was your grandmother's, and I thought you might have a need for it."

Hesitantly, Cole held out his own hand, curious what his father had for him, but knowing he was asking for forgiveness and trying to make things right again.

Roy grasped Cole's hand, then placed what he was holding on his palm and curled Cole's fingers around it. "Take good care of her," he said, briefly making eye contact.

"Thanks, Dad." Cole hadn't called him that in so long it made his eyes dampen. And if he looked at the old cowboy in front of him, he knew he'd likely see the same moisture. He focused on their cupped hands, trying to make his next words strong instead of quavering with emotion. "I will."

Roy squeezed Cole's closed fist, then paused for a split second before letting go. Tipping his cowboy hat, he turned and walked to his truck without looking back.

Cole opened his hand and gazed at the small, worn ring box. Fresh starts built on the strength of the past.

EPILOGUE

Jackie couldn't believe how quickly her friends had packed up her San Antonio apartment and got her situated at the Sweet Meadows Ranch.

The Wylder clan had folded in around her, making sure her father didn't lose his reserved spot in the Sweet Hills Memory Care Facility. She'd never been fussed over so thoroughly in all her life, and knew it wasn't just because she was a Wylder-to-be. They were her family and had been for years.

It looked like chasing Cole all her life had paid off in more ways than one.

Levi had offered to clear out the office that had once been Cole's room, so she could stay in it. But knowing she wouldn't spend a single night in there—at least not alone—she told him it was fine; she'd bunk with Cole in Brant's old room. Then she'd given Cole a gigantic kiss in case anyone had missed the fact that the two of them were stepping down their own little path to a happily ever after.

Myles had rolled his eyes and declared he was moving out.

It had been a month so far, and he hadn't yet. Each morning at breakfast, Jackie asked if today was the day he'd propose to Karen. So far he hadn't done that yet, either.

But she knew it was coming soon, just like the small pre-built home she and Cole had on order and would sit on the other side of the holly hedge, next door to Carmichael's.

As for Ryan, he was over at Carly's more nights than he was at the ranch. It looked like something might be brewing there, too.

Jackie and Goose had blended right into ranch life, making themselves at home as well as useful when Owen Lancaster had unexpectedly quit. She hadn't been able to pry anything out of the former hired hand other than that he'd been made an offer he couldn't refuse, and she'd soon hear all about it.

As for Goose, he wasn't much of a herding dog, but he was definitely happier running with the other dogs, dragging grass and dust into the house in his shaggy coat each evening.

And Cole's new puppy from Brant had eaten only about a third of her footwear so far, so the young lab-retriever was learning. A bit slowly for her liking, though.

From the ranch Jackie was only a twenty-two-minute drive from her father, who had settled in fairly easily, charming the staff and already taming a squirrel to eat out of his hand when he sat under the ground's large oaks.

He was doing well, and so was she.

And so was Cole.

Soon they would pick a date for their wedding and things would get crazy with preparations. She hoped he was prepared for a gigantic event with everyone she knew helping them celebrate.

She had finally found her happily ever after, the love of her life, and she hoped that during the coming football season she could find that same love for her friends Jenny, Violet and Daisy-Mae.

Because everyone deserved love like she and Cole had.

She hadn't gone back to her job at the feed store, instead

finding a position with the community college's breeding study. The mayor and his wife Donna were delighted, handing her boxes of paperwork that they'd been managing, and Jackie had gladly dug in. Spending time with Cole, Levi, Brant and April on the project while out in the Texas sun worked well for her. She didn't miss sitting at a desk, although she missed the constant interruption of townsfolk clomping up the stairs to stop by her office.

Then again, she'd told everyone on the ranch that auction day—every second Friday—was important to her new job, and they could find her in the diner those mornings. She'd be there picking brains and eavesdropping on various ranchers talking about breeding bulls. It was really just an excuse to enjoy Mrs. Fisher's special pie of the day and get her fill of people.

As well, several days a week she found herself there with Cole, sitting at the back counter enjoying a Wylder special and starting new rumors around town. Sort of like this morning.

She lifted her cup of coffee as their meals arrived, and Cole raised his, clinking it against hers in a well-practiced toast. She took a sip, then set her cup down and leaned over, kissing her fiancé. The kiss turned deeper and Mrs. Fisher cleared her throat.

"A kiss like that? Hmm." Garfield Goodwin raised his bushy white eyebrows at Mrs. Fisher. "Takes you back, doesn't it?"

The waitress turned to him. "You and I never kissed, Garfield."

"Not for my lack of trying," he teased.

She gave him a stern frown. "Have you met my twin sister? She lives in Dallas." She pointed to a woman sitting at the end of the counter, who had similar blond hair piled high and the same perky energy.

Garfield pivoted on his stool, eyes widening.

"She's single and has heard a lot about you," Mrs. Fisher said, as her sister turned their way, her smile big and bright.

Garfield's eyes sparkled as he slipped off his stool and stepped toward her, extending his hand. "Garfield Goodwin at your service, my dear."

"The pleasure is all mine," the woman purred. "Are you single, honey?"

"I've been waiting all my life for the right woman to come walking through that diner door. Want to join me for lunch and see if you're her?"

Mrs. Fisher's sister allowed Garfield to lead her to their own table near the front of the restaurant.

From her spot on the stool beside Jackie, Daisy-Mae rolled her eyes. "Seriously? Is Cupid ever going to find me in this town or do I need to move somewhere else?"

"He'll find you," Jackie assured her. "I can feel it."

"Can I make a request? Because I have my eye on someone."

Jackie sucked in an excited breath. "Tell me!"

"No way." Her friend lowered her eyebrows. "You can still work your matchmaking magic without me telling you who it is."

Jackie nodded, fairly certain she knew exactly who Daisy-Mae had set her sights on. A guy who would knock her socks off.

Cole wrapped his arm around Jackie. "It's a good thing I sat behind you at all those games, isn't it? Imagine how lonely we'd be otherwise."

She laughed, leaning her head against his shoulder. "You know, I was thinking..."

He gave her a quick kiss as she straightened again.

"If you like me, Cole Wylder, you may as well walk me down the aisle soon and save yourself starting rumors that you're stringing me along."

He gave her an incredulous look. "It hasn't even been a month!" He held out her hand, displaying the antique ring on her finger. "And I got you a ring within twenty-four hours of proposing."

"Thanks to your father," Jackie said with a smile.

Cole sighed, acting as though he was put out.

"Now, a wedding sounds like a fine plan," Mrs. Fisher said, as she came by again with her coffeepot. "If you start planning now, you could have a lovely fall wedding." She topped up Jackie's cup while eyeing her midriff, on the lookout for a baby bump.

Jackie rubbed her stomach, saying, "Not yet, Mrs. Fisher. I plan to do things in order."

"Well, don't wait too long. We could use some excitement around here now that all the Wylder boys have finally found love. We need someone to start working on the next generation of folks to fill this diner. You know what I mean?" the waitress asked, eyeing Jackie again.

"I think that's a brilliant idea, and I might know just the woman for the job," Jackie declared.

"You do?" Cole asked, looking a bit pale.

"I do." She leaned in, giving him a long sweet kiss that was full of happily ever after.

When they broke apart, he was smiling. "Can I order a set of twins? I've always thought they'd be fun."

Jackie laughed. Some men were worth waiting for. And sometimes real life was even better than some dusty old fantasy crush.

THE COWBOY'S OF SWEETHEART CREEK, TEXAS

Read them all!

The Cowboy's Stolen Heart (Levi)

The Cowboy's Secret Wish (Myles)

The Cowboy's Second Chance (Ryan)

The Cowboy's Sweet Elopement (Brant)

The Cowboy's Surprise Return (Cole)

There are more Sweetheart Creek stories set in Indigo Bay! Maria has her own special story, Sweet Joymaker. Their cousin Nick's story is Sweet Troublemaker. And you can't forget about the Wylders' cousin Alexa! Her story is Sweet Holiday Surprise.

Indigo Bay

Sweet romances set in a beach town—meet characters new and old in this spinoff series.

Sweet Matchmaker (Ginger and Logan)

Sweet Holiday Surprise (Cash & Alexa)

Sweet Forgiveness (Ashton & Zoe)

Sweet Troublemaker (Nick & Polly)

Sweet Joymaker (Maria & Clint)

VEILS AND VOWS

The Promise (Book 0: Devon & Olivia)

The Surprise Wedding (Book 1: Devon & Olivia)

A Pinch of Commitment (Book 2: Ethan & Lily)

The Wedding Plan (Book 3: Luke & Emma)

Accidentally Married (Book 4: Burke & Jill)

The Marriage Pledge (Book 5: Moe & Amy)

Mail Order Soulmate (Book 6: Zach & Catherine)

ALSO BY JEAN ORAM

Have you fallen in love with Blueberry Springs? Catch up with your friends and their adventures...

Book 1: Whiskey and Gumdrops (Mandy & Frankie)

Book 2: Rum and Raindrops (Jen & Rob)

Book 3: Eggnog and Candy Canes (Katie & Nash)

Book 4: Sweet Treats (3 short stories—Mandy, Amber, & Nicola)

Book 5: Vodka and Chocolate Drops (Amber & Scott)

Book 6: Tequila and Candy Drops (Nicola & Todd)

Companion Novel: Champagne and Lemon Drops (Beth & Oz)

THE SUMMER SISTERS

Taming billionaires has never been so *sweet*. If you adored the Wylders, be sure to check out this family saga as well!

** Available in paperback & ebook & audio! **

One cottage. Four sisters. And four billionaires who will sweep them off their feet.

Falling for the Movie Star

Falling for the Boss

Falling for the Single Dad

Falling for the Bodyguard

Falling for the Firefighter

ABOUT THE AUTHOR

Jean Oram is a *New York Times* and *USA Today* bestselling romance author. Inspiration for her small town series came from her own upbringing on the Canadian prairies. Although, so far, none of her characters have grown up in an old schoolhouse or worked on a bee farm. Jean still lives on the prairie with her husband, two kids, and big shaggy dog where she can be found out playing in the snow or hiking.

Become an Official Fan:
www.facebook.com/groups/jeanoramfans
Newsletter: www.jeanoram.com/FREEBOOK
Twitter: www.twitter.com/jeanoram
Instagram: www.instagram.com/author_jeanoram
Facebook: www.facebook.com/JeanOramAuthor
Website & blog: www.jeanoram.com

CPSIA information can be obtained
at www.ICGtesting.com
Printed in the USA
BVHW031427240221
600996BV00002B/134

9 781989 359396